WANTED

by

Maggie Carpenter

Cover

Dark Secrets Press

Published by: Dark Secrets Press
Visit Maggie Carpenter
http://www.MaggieCarpenter.com
https://www.facebook.com/MaggieCarpenterWriter
https://twitter.com/magcarpenter2

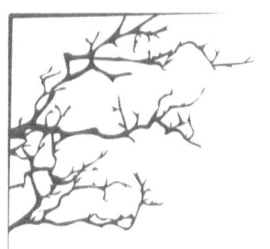

PROLOGUE

TESS GLANCED AT THE clock. Fifteen minutes and she could lock the door and head home. The wind had whipped up, the rain was starting, and she couldn't imagine anyone stopping into her small cafe at such a late hour, but as she began wiping down the counters she heard the jingle of the bell over the door.

A rush of icy air made her shiver.

"I'll be with you in a minute," she called. "You just caught me. I'm about to close up."

The scraping of the stool behind her told her the visitor had chosen to sit at the counter. Automatically grabbing the coffee pot and a mug she turned to greet him, but the man's head was down, a black cowboy hat hiding his face, and his elbows resting on the counter.

But his hands made her catch her breath.

They reminded her of the hands that had once held hers.

Hands about which she had fantasized, imagining how they might feel if they ever explored her body.

Hands, that, however lightly they once touched her, had never failed to make her skin tingle.

But the man couldn't possibly be *him*.

Her pulse racing, she set down the mug and poured the coffee. Without lifting his head he reached for the cream, dropped in a splash, added three packets of sugar, then slowly stirred the rich, brown beverage.

She watched, like a deer in headlights, as he lifted the mug it to his thick, full lips.

"You've got a choice."

1

Her heart leapt.

The rich baritone voice was unmistakable.

Her eyes darted to the door, terrified someone would enter, and though a thousand questions spun through her head her voice refused to work.

"You can pick up the phone and call your brother," he continued, "or you can let me sit here a spell and listen to what I have to say."

The desperate need to scream at him for sweeping back into her life was battling with the thudding need to leap across the counter, throw her arms around his neck, and hug him until the sun came up.

"Not callin'? That's good. So is this coffee, just like I remember. Real good."

She watched him straighten up, then slowly lift his head. As his hazel eyes caught hers, she tried to swallow back the heat in her throat.

It only burned hotter.

"I've been thinkin' about this moment every day since I was sent up," he drawled, then staring at her intently he let out a heavy sigh. "Damn! I swear you're even more beautiful now than when I left."

Whiskers lined his jaw, dirt-filled creases crossed his face—creases she didn't remember him having—and a scar sat above his right eyebrow. His broad shoulders struggled to break through the seams of his tight jacket, and the denim fabric was too thin for the wintry weather.

"You have no right to say that," she stammered, "and why, Luke, why did you come back, and why did you come here, to my cafe? Are you crazy?"

"Maybe, Tess, but I've gotta clear my name," he replied, then tilting his head and narrowing his eyes he added, "and I need to get you back, darlin', along with our life, or at least the promise of our life. We'd barely gotten off the ground. I'm not lettin' that go."

"What life? A few dates? That's not a life, and besides, that horse has left the barn," she muttered with a deep frown, trying to ignore the intense need to fall into his arms and sink against his chest.

"Nothin's impossible, and we were somethin' special. In my book we still are," he declared, then pausing and lowering his voice, he murmured, "In your heart you know I didn't do what they said."

"What do you want me to—?"

But headlights suddenly shone through the windows.

Her heart thundering, she squinted to see if she could recognize the car. The row of lights on the roof told her exactly who it was.

"Oh, no! Jeb."

"Dammit. That pesky brother of yours always did have bad timin'," Luke growled.

"Hurry, go in the back."

"You're gonna help me?" he asked, a surprised half-smile crossing his lips.

"I don't know what I'm going to do yet," she retorted, "but I don't need to deal with Jeb walking in and finding you sitting at my counter. For pity's sake, will you just get in the back?"

"I guess I'd better."

Quickly grabbing his coffee as he slid off the stool, he headed towards the kitchen. Trying to control her panic, her eyes moved from him, to the window, then back to him as he disappeared through the swinging doors.

LEANING AGAINST THE wall, Luke Larson pulled off his hat and let out a heavy breath. After being on the run for three days he was exhausted, starving, and bone-cold. He'd stolen the clothes from a dry cleaning van, and while they'd served their purpose, they were a size too small and offered little protection. But he couldn't worry about such details. The clanging of the bell over the door told him Jeb Turner had walked in. Tess's brother had been against him from the get-go.

"Hey, Jeb, you want some coffee?" he heard Tess ask. "Why are you here so late?"

"Thought I'd better warn you," her brother replied. "You might wanna prepare yourself. Luke Larson escaped and there's a good chance he might be headed this way."

"Really?" she said, her voice feigning surprise. "How did that happen?"

"How? He's just a real smart character, always was," Jeb grunted. "Got himself a job in some kinda vegetable garden near the outer fence and gave the guards the slip."

"Don't you think that sounds a bit fishy?"

"Yep, sure does, but like I said, Luke always was a crafty fella."

"Why did it take three days for you to hear about it?"

"There's the real question, and we still haven't been able to get an answer, but it doesn't matter, the bastard is out!" Jeb exclaimed. "Tess, you listen, and you listen good. If he shows up or contacts you, you've gotta call me, you understand?"

"Jeb, you may be the deputy sheriff and my big brother, but I don't appreciate you taking that tone with me."

"He had some kinda spell on you, and if he comes back and you help him and get yourself caught, I won't be able to get you outta trouble. I'm just lookin' out for you, that's all."

"I'm a big girl!"

"Damn, you're as obstinate as you were when you were just a little kid in socks," he scolded. "I mean it, Tess, don't you be messin' with him, you hear?"

"I have to close up," she said, ignoring his strident warning. "Buzz off and let me finish my chores."

"You might be shuttin' your door, but I'm on duty," he barked, "and the sheriff said I've gotta look around this place, so..."

"Fine, do what you have to, but make it quick. I want to go home."

To Luke's dismay, the kitchen offered nowhere to hide. Creeping forward to the rear door that led to the storeroom, he opened it slowly, afraid it might creak. It didn't, and saying a quick prayer of thanks he moved inside.

Turning on the light, he closed the door behind him and stared across the large space. His heart sank. It was barren except for some empty boxes and an old freezer. He shook his head. Tess had bought it for next to nothing, swearing it would be a bargain even after paying to have it repaired. It sat silent, still inoperative.

"Damn, I can't believe you've still got this thing," he muttered, hurrying across to it.

Lifting the lid, an ugly smell wafted around him, but a second scan of the room told him it was his only choice. Racing back to turn off the light switch, he found his way through the dark, and climbed into the foul smelling, empty freezer.

IN THE KITCHEN, JEB had spied the half empty mug of coffee sitting near the sink. Picking it up, he eyed Tess suspiciously.

"What's this? Why is it still hot?"

"Jeez, Jeb, this is a cafe. I had a customer who left in a hurry and I brought it back in here to wash."

"A customer in a hurry? Luke Larson perhaps?"

"You're being ridiculous. What's wrong with you?"

"Sorry, sis," he said, his voice softening. "I've just got a gut feelin' he'll try to see you. It'd be just like him to wander in here late at night."

"You're right about one thing," she said impatiently, "it's late."

"Okay, okay! I'll take a quick look in the storeroom and be on my way."

"Please hurry, I'm tired. I've been on my feet for hours and I want go home."

Moving across to the door and pushing it open, he flipped up the light switch and looked across the empty space.

Cowering behind him Tess was petrified. When they'd walked into the kitchen and Luke was gone, the only place he could be was the storeroom, but as her worried eyes scrutinized the area, it appeared to be empty. There was no way out except through the back door to the alley, but that was locked. She couldn't understand how he had vanished into thin air.

"When are you gonna lose that freezer?" Jeb asked brusquely. "You've had that damn thing for ages."

"I don't know," she replied with a shrug. "Max said he'd have it running soon. Please can we go now?"

"Max," Jeb growled, turning off the light and closing the door. "That guy couldn't make a horse run ten feet."

"That doesn't even make any sense," she exclaimed, rolling her eyes as she followed him to the front of the cafe.

"Remember what I said," he warned, abruptly stopping and shaking his finger at her.

"Enough!"

Sighing heavily and shaking his head, he walked across the empty dining room, but paused when he reached the door.

"Make sure you—"

"Jeb, please!"

"Hey, easy, I was just going to say, make sure you use the dead bolt. With Larson on the loose, you can't be too careful."

"Oh, sorry," she said sheepishly. "Like I said, I'm really tired."

"Then get outta here and get some rest. You know I love you."

"I know, I know, I love you too, but jeez you're a pain in the ass sometimes."

"Right back at ya, sis. Damn, it's cold tonight," he muttered, opening the door.

Locking it behind him, Tess watched through the window as he climbed into his squad car and headed into the street.

Light snow flurries were starting.

It would be a cold, wintry night.

Pulling down the shade and hurrying back to the storeroom, she opened the door and turned on the lights.

"Luke, where the hell are you?"

She heard a faint pounding, and it took her a minute before she realized it was coming from the freezer.

"I don't believe it," she exclaimed rushing across the room.

"Wow, I'm real glad you heard me," he groaned, uncurling his body as she lifted the lid. "That was a tight fit, and I couldn't get the damn thing open."

In the bright, fluorescent light, Tess could see the strain in his face and the dark circles around his eyes.

Her stomach churned.

Though she hated to admit it, she was still crazy about him.

But he'd betrayed her.

The buried anger suddenly surfaced.

"Dammit, Luke, you shouldn't have come here."

"I had to," he replied, his voice low and deadly serious, "but before we get into all the shit, I need a long, hot shower, a decent meal, then sleep. Hours of sleep. Sleep until I wake up."

"I don't know how—"

"Then," he interrupted, "you're gonna sit still and let me explain a few things. After I'm done you can do whatever you want. Turn me in, let me loose, or help me. If you don't wanna call Jeb, but you don't wanna help me either, I'll leave, and you'll never hear from me again."

"But, Luke," she said, her head spinning and her heart filled with conflict, "even if I wanted to take you home, how can I? I'm sure Jeb will be on the lookout."

"Hey, like your brother said, I'm a crafty fella!"

"Yes, you are," she quipped, the first hint of a smile on her lips. "You convinced me to go out with you even though everyone was against it."

The shared memory sparkled between them, and she felt her anger beginning to fade. But a worried frown suddenly crossed her brow. Though she had found the accusations hard to believe, Jeb had convinced her.

Had she been wrong?

Was Luke innocent after all?

"I know a way you can get me into your house," he said softly, "if you want." "If I want," she murmured, suddenly flashing back to the time he'd said those same three words before...*I'll spank you properly, but only if you want.*

Standing before him in the cold storeroom, it was as if no time had passed. She could feel the dampness between her legs, and the hot flush crawl up her neck and move over her face.

Luke Larson was a drug.

She was addicted.

She always had been.

"Tell me what I have to do," she whispered, wishing the butterflies in her stomach would settle.

"Thank you, Tess," he purred, his sultry voice sending her goosebumps popping. "First thing, we gotta take care of Dudley Do Right. I expect he's sittin' in his car at the end of the alley. He's gonna watch and see if you come out alone and then follow you home."

"Dudley Do Right?"

"Hey, if the shoe fits," Luke said with a devilish grin. "Now listen carefully and do exactly what I tell you."

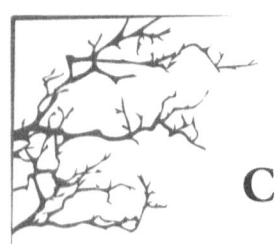

CHAPTER ONE

JEB TURNER WAS EXACTLY where Luke had predicted. Sitting at the end of the alley parked in the shadows. Jeb knew his sister, and she'd been hiding something. It didn't mean that *something* was Luke Larson, but Luke had escaped custody, and that was reason enough for Jeb to keep a close eye on his sister.

Strumming his fingers against the steering wheel as he hummed the melody to a recent country hit, he wondered why she was taking so long to leave. He was about to call and make sure she was okay when the back door opened and she stepped outside. Even in the bad weather, the bright overhead lamp made her clearly visible. Studying her as she unlocked her car, everything appeared perfectly normal, but she unexpectedly hurried back indoors. A moment later his cell phone rang. He instinctively knew it was her, and let out a grunt when her name on his screen confirmed it.

"Tess, what's up?"

"Are you still close by? I need your help."

"Sure. What's happened? Are you okay?"

"It's no big deal. I forgot to get down one of those large cans of coffee. I need to leave it out for the morning crew and I've already put away the ladder. It's a pain to bring it back out."

"No problem. I'll be right there."

Not wanting her to know he'd been watching from the alley, he decided to circle the block before rolling into the parking area in front of the cafe.

THOUGH SHE WAS ANXIOUS, Tess had no second thoughts about conning her brother. The handsome man standing in front of her, the man who had once stolen her heart, had risked life and limb to reach her. He deserved the chance to tell his story.

But she knew that wasn't the only reason for the choice she'd made.

Jeb had been right.

Luke's magic spell was irresistible.

"He's on his way," she said, fetching a blanket from a storage cupboard.

"Great. Remember, stay calm."

"I know, you don't have to worry. Come on, let's get out of here before he arrives."

Moving through the storeroom and out the exit to her car, she opened the back door. Climbing in and laying on the floor, she covered him with the thick, wool blanket.

"Man, this is great," he said grinning up at her. "This is the warmest I've been in three days," then lowering his voice, he added, "Thank you, Tess. You won't regret this."

"That remains to be seen," she murmured, but the edge was gone from her voice.

She suddenly felt sorry for him.

If he really was innocent...

"Tess, you need to get back inside."

Abruptly realizing she'd been staring at him, she wordlessly closed the door and hurried away. Moving quickly through the storeroom and kitchen, she entered the cafe just as headlights blazed through the windows. Opening up, an unexpected blast of freezing air swirled around her as she watched Jeb's tall frame march towards her.

"Damn. Sure has gotten nasty quick," he remarked, walking past her and heading towards the kitchen.

"The coffee can is on the top shelf next to the refrigerator."

Hurrying after him as he entered the kitchen, she stood back as he lifted his long arms, brought it down, and placed it on the counter.

"There you go," he declared. "Do you need help with anything else while I'm here?"

"Actually...I've been thinking about what you said. If Luke comes back to town he'll probably try to see me."

"Well, good! I'm glad you're startin' to think straight."

"Do you think you could follow me home and make sure the house is empty before I go in?"

"Sure can, and I'm real glad you want me to. I was gonna offer earlier, but you were gettin' a bit rat-assed."

"Must you use that term? You know I hate it."

"Hey, I call it like I see it, and you were," he replied, raising his eyebrows, "but that's okay. You've settled down and that's the main thing. Follow me to your house, and then wait in your garage until I come in and give you the all clear."

"Perfect, thanks, Jeb," she said, pecking him on the cheek and handing him her house key. "You can be a nice brother when you want to be."

"You know what you need?"

"I should," she quipped, rolling her eyes. "You've told me enough times."

"It bears repeatin'. A good man with a firm hand."

"And you need a good woman with a rolling pin to clonk you over the head," she exclaimed, grabbing his arm and pushing him out of the kitchen and through the cafe.

Waiting until he was safely settled behind the wheel, she bolted out the door, hurried to the exit, then struggled the short distance through the wind-blown snow to her waiting car.

"You okay back there?" she panted as she climbed in.

"I feel great," he replied, moving the blanket off his face to answer. "This is so warm I could sleep here all night, but why are you out of breath?"

"Can't you hear it? The storm's picked up. For once I'm glad my overly-protective brother is escorting me home."

"Just be careful. I won't stay hidden for long if you skid off the road and plow into a tree!"

"You don't have to remind me," she muttered, starting up the car and driving cautiously forward.

It was a short trip, but the roads were icy, and Jeb drove slowly. Finally turning into her driveway and rolling into her garage, she glanced through the back window. Jeb had parked at the curb and was trudging up the path to her front door, his long coat flapping and his head down. As he disappeared inside, she lowered the garage door, and turned on the interior car lights.

"Won't be long now, Luke," she said softly. "This was a clever idea."

"I have them from time to time."

"Uh, Luke?"

"Yeah?"

"Was it bad in there?"

"Prison?"

"Uh-huh."

He paused.

"That bad?" she pressed. "You don't have to talk about it if you don't want to."

"Let's just say it wasn't a picnic on the riverbank."

She was searching for a response when the door leading into the house opened, flooding the garage with light.

"Shit. Jeb's here. Cover your head," she said hastily, then climbed out and walked up to meet her brother.

"Here are your keys," he declared, handing them to her. "Everything looks good, but call me if you need to, and I mean any time."

"Thanks."

"I'm gonna have Dwayne drive around the neighborhood, then park down the street and keep watch."

"Dwayne?" she said skeptically.

"He's a nice kid, even if he is a bit on the slow side. A stakeout like this will be good experience, and his uncle will appreciate it."

"If it helps you with the sheriff, it's fine by me."

"Talk to you tomorrow. Let me out this way," he suggested, gesturing towards the garage door.

"Okay," she said, not wanting to argue.

Hitting the button on the wall to open it up, she prayed Luke was completely under the blanket as Jeb marched past. With a final wave, he broke into a jog, but she waited until he drove away before closing down the door.

"Luke, he's gone," she said softly, poking her head inside the car. "We can go inside."

Slowly sitting up, then climbing out, he stretched his body as he stared down at her with weary eyes.

"You look done in," she murmured, shocked at the redness in his eyes. "Do you want to just go to bed?"

"No, I need to shower and eat, or eat and shower."

"I have left over chicken and dumplings. It will take about fifteen minutes to heat up."

"Then I guess it's a shower first," he declared with a yawn, then shivered as a chill rattled through his bones.

"You'd better come in." she said quickly. "It's freezing in here."

"There were days I thought I'd never see this place again," he murmured, following her into the house and down the hall. "You know," he added, his voice husky, "you're savin' my life right now."

"I don't know about that," she replied, unable to think of anything else to say. "You'll find everything you need in the bathroom, and you can use the robe hanging on the hook by the shower. It's Jeb's, so it should fit."

Opening the door to the guest room, she stared up at his handsome, rugged face, and the untamable lock of hair falling over his right eye.

A pang of regret pierced her heart.

Energy crackled between them.

His fingertip unexpectedly touched her forehead, then slowly traced around her face to her chin.

She caught her breath.

"I've done that a thousand times in my mind," he said softly, then holding her eyes for a fleeting moment, he turned and walked into the bedroom.

Fighting the intense pull to follow him, she hurried to the kitchen, placed the casserole dish in the microwave, then dropped into a chair at the kitchen table. Willing her heart to settle, she thought back to their last evening together.

He'd told her he'd spank her if she didn't stop punching his arm. The challenge was too exciting to pass up, and she'd thumped again—twice—her eyes blazing back at him.

"I take it you want me to spank you," he'd said with a grin.

"You wouldn't dare!"

He'd immediately pulled her out of the car, bent her over the hood, and slapped her backside over her thin skirt. Though deeply embarrassed, a vibrant heat had surged through her sex.

"I keep my promises, Tess Turner," he declared, straightening her up and wrapping her in his arms.

She was ready to invite him home for a late night drink, but he'd abruptly released her, saying he had to leave. She'd understood. A rumor had begun circulating in the small town. Luke's truck had been seen in the area of a gas station burglary. Old man Nate, the elderly attendant, had been attacked, and the cash register emptied.

"God only knows what's gonna happen with this robbery business," he'd said solemnly, "but until things simmer down it's best we keep our distance. I hope you'll keep your faith in me."

Sighing at the memory of his words, a wave of guilt moved through her heart. Then she remembered the lie he'd told.

A rush of anger surged through her body.

"Man that smells good!"

His voice snatched her attention.

Lifting her gaze, she could hardly believe how different he looked. Wrapped in the thick, dark brown, terry cloth robe, clean-shaven and his face scrubbed clean, he looked like himself again.

But flooded with fury, she jumped to her feet.

"Why did you lie to me?" she demanded. "You said you were through with Patty Jamison!"

His eyes narrowed, but what she saw wasn't scorn, it was confusion.

"Say something!"

Abruptly lunging forward, he grabbed her tightly around the waist, walked her backwards, and pressed her against the wall.

"Dammit woman. If you'd given me a chance to explain—"

"Explain?" she interrupted, her voice shrill, her faced crunched as she blazed at him. "What's there to explain?"

"You need a spankin'," he said solemnly, "a real good spankin'."

"What kind of a thing is that to say right now?"

"You're all wound up, and it seems like you have been for a while. I saw it the minute I looked at your face across that counter in the cafe. You've never made sense of the crap that happened."

"I don't know what you're talking about," she lied, "and besides, I'm with Tyler now."

The son of a wealthy rancher, Tyler had been no friend to him, but the fabrication didn't have the effect she wanted. Luke's lips curled in an odd smile.

"Is that right?" he asked lightly, then moved his mouth to her ear. "Does Tyler smack that beautiful bottom of yours when you're bein' a brat? Does he hold you like I once did?" Then jerking his head back, he locked her eyes. "Why would you make up a foolish tale like that?"

"It's not a tale, it's—"

"Stop lyin'," he growled, cutting her off. "Why'd you say that?"

"Because, uh, I wanted to hurt you like you hurt me."

Though heat moved through her throat, she held his gaze.

"You know I didn't do what they said, any of it," he muttered, "and when I, uh, when I..."

A strange look crossed his face, and abruptly releasing her, he brought his hands up to his head.

"Luke, what is it?"

"I'm kinda dizzy," he answered, stepping away and stumbling into a chair. "I reckon no food or sleep for three days will do that."

"Shit, I'm so sorry."

Grabbing a plate from the cupboard, she removed the casserole from the microwave, dished up a large helping of the steaming chicken and dumplings, and placed it in front of him.

"While you're eating that, I'll make us some coffee, but eat slowly," she said, fetching him a knife and fork. "Devouring food on an empty stomach can make you sick."

"Thanks, darlin'," he murmured, taking a mouthful. "Damn, this is mighty good."

"Uh, I think I believe you," she whispered, a hot flush crossing her face. "I mean, that you didn't do all those things, except for Patty. You were with her."

His hazel eyes lifted.

"But you don't know why, and after I was arrested you refused to talk to me."

"I'm sorry. It was a confusing time," she stammered, "and I didn't say I did believe you, I said *I think* I believe you."

"That's a start," he said, pausing between mouthfuls of his meal. "I know a lotta people kept tellin' you I was a bad guy, and the evidence wasn't helpin.'" Then breaking into a grin, he added, "There were days I even wondered about myself."

"How can you joke around? You've been through hell."

"Gotta keep a positive attitude, especially when things are bad," he replied, "but I've got it figured out, and if I'm right, it's just as well you turned against me."

"I don't understand."

"You will, but I have to eat and sleep before I can get into it."

"I'm sorry. You're right. I can be horribly impatient."

"That's why you need a spankin,'" he remarked, continuing to eat but staring straight at her. "A proper spankin', not a few slaps on the backside over your dress."

She dropped her eyes.

His threat had sent a bevy of butterflies fluttering in her stomach, and a hot flood through her sex.

She still loved him.

She'd never stopped.

CHAPTER TWO

LUKE'S SLEEP HAD BEEN deep and dreamless, but he jerked awake. His heart punched his chest. For a moment he had no idea where he was, but as he took in the familiar guest room, he sank back into the comfortable mattress.

"I will never take a delicious meal and a soft bed for granted again," he muttered. "Thank God, for you, Tess."

Closing his eyes, he imagined her just down the hall. Though he'd been crazy about her for years, he'd convinced himself she was out of his league. He was a small time rancher, and her father one of the town's wealthiest citizens. But one day the thought of being in her company was just too tempting, and he'd stopped into her cafe for lunch.

To his delight and surprise, she'd joined him for a chat.

He'd lost himself in her large blue eyes, and found himself laughing at her witty comments. When she'd stood up and cleared away his plates, he knew she was the one. He became determined to win her over.

Now lying in the guest room, surrounded by the warm memory and dark stillness, he dropped his hand to his cock and pictured her next to him, her soft, yielding body naked and wanting. He could almost feel her as he imagined his fingers tracing her spine, then rolling her on to her back, and moving his fingers into her sex.

His mind jumped.

He was tickling her clit with his tongue, slipping his hands under her backside to lift her hips, and lapping her sweetness until her moans became cries of orgasmic ecstasy.

Trying to control the volume of his groans, he clenched his teeth as his cock spewed over his hand. Taking a moment to catch his breath, he staggered to the bathroom, wiped himself clean, then returned to bed, praying for the opportunity to make things right with the woman he loved.

IN HER BEDROOM, TESS was wide awake. She wasn't sure what had caused her to stir, but unable to go back to sleep she moved quietly from the bed, wrapping her robe tightly around her body. Padding into the kitchen and pouring herself a glass of milk, she set it in the microwave to heat. The small task reminded her of her mother.

"I miss you, mom," she whispered to the air. "I miss your wisdom and the way you used to make everything seem okay even when it wasn't."

The microwave beeped.

Removing the hot glass, she wandered into the living room and peered through the narrow crack in the curtains. The patrol car parked across the street was no surprise, and sipping her milk, she tried to think of a way to make her brother back off. Suddenly weary and letting out a long yawn, she left the empty glass on the coffee table and returned to bed, but rolling on her side, she felt the presence of the man down the hall.

When he'd wandered into her cafe for lunch all those months before, she could scarcely believe it. She'd always found the cowboy from the other side of town intriguing. She was drawn to his powerful physique, and whenever she saw him in town he'd be cracking jokes. Deciding to take the bull by the horns she'd sat down to say hello, and quickly found herself mesmerized by his smoldering dark eyes. When he'd called and asked her out, she'd accepted, and by the end of dinner at an intimate restaurant just outside town, he had stolen her heart.

Then it all went wrong.

Old man Nate was attacked and robbed, and her father, her brother, and even Tyler, had damned Luke. Initially she'd defended him, but when his alibi was Patty Jamison, the woman he'd sworn he'd stopped seeing, she'd felt betrayed.

Sighing sadly, she realized she'd been wrong to go along with his accusers so easily. He'd tried to talk to her, but egged on by her father and Jeb, she'd refused.

Her eyes closed, she dozed off, and barely had she fallen asleep when her cell phone rang. Groggily opening her eyes, she looked at the screen.

"Jeb," she muttered testily, snatching it from the nights.

"Hey, easy there. I just wanted to make sure everything's okay."

"I was sound asleep. Why are you calling so early? You know I left the cafe late."

"Tess, it's almost ten o'clock."

"That's early for me," she retorted. "Please wait until at least eleven from now on."

"Okay, hon," he said patiently. "I'll remember."

"Thank you, and was that Barney Fife across the street from my house last night?"

"Stop calling him that," Jeb said, irritation creeping into his voice. "Dwayne is a good cop, and I told you he'd be there."

"I know, but when I saw him I couldn't help thinking what would happen if he did come across Luke? Do you honestly think he'd have a chance of lasting more than two-seconds? He couldn't even bring in that thirteen-year-old who was fishing without a license! You're not doing him any favors posted out there."

"He's smart enough to call for back-up, and a squad car opposite your house is a deterrent."

"Fine, whatever," she said with a resigned sigh. "I was worried last night, but I'm not anymore, and this nanny nonsense will drive me crazy."

"It won't be for long. The law will be catchin' up with Luke Larson pretty quick. I've gotta run. Go back to sleep."

"Like that's going to happen," she mumbled under her breath. "Okay, Jeb, I'll talk to you later."

Ending the call, she stretched out and yawned, forgetting about her brother, and thinking how marvelous it would be to wake up next to Luke.

"I'd love to share a whole morning in bed with you," she breathed, and dropping her fingers against her sex, she let her mind take flight.

"Tess, I told you I'm gonna spank your butt, and I keep my promises."

"You're not gonna spank me hard, are you?"

"What's my first rule of spankin'?"

"You'll spank me as hard and as long as you see fit."

Rubbing herself vigorously, she could feel her climax building, and as she pictured herself over his knee, his large, hard hand slapping her naked backside, the orgasm seized her, sending sparkling spasms shuddering through her body.

A SHORT TIME LATER, wrapped in the robe he'd found hanging on the bathroom door, Luke wandered into the kitchen. He smiled. The delicious aroma of sizzling bacon wafted around him. It was one he'd not enjoyed for some time.

"It smells as good as your chicken and dumplings, maybe even better."

Turning around, he saw her eyes fall on his exposed chest, but quickly darting her gaze up to his face, she greeted him with a warm smile. He immediately sensed a change in her demeanor.

"I don't think I've ever seen anyone as tired as you were last night," she remarked. "I hope you slept well."

"I can't begin to tell you how well, and it seems you did too. You sure look a lot happier this mornin'."

"That's because I am!" she declared. "Take a seat."

Walking up to the kitchen table, he settled into a chair, and watched as she dished up the breakfast.

"Here you go," she said, placing the scrambled eggs and bacon in front of him. "I can rustle up more if that's not enough."

"Thank you, Tess. This looks great," he exclaimed, eyeing it hungrily as he picked up his fork.

She poured them both a mug of coffee, dished out the remainder on a plate for herself, then sat across from him.

"Tess, that has to be the best damn coffee on the planet," he said gratefully, taking a long drink. "I'm beginnin' to feel almost normal. I'm sorry if I shocked you last night. There was no easy way to approach you."

"Can you tell your side of the story now, and would you mind starting with Patty Jamison?"

"Sure, as soon as I finish this great grub."

"If you give me the clothes you were wearing, I can throw them in the wash for you."

"I'd be much obliged, but they're way too small. I need to get back to my ranch and pick up a few things," he said between mouthfuls, "and I've gotta talk to Robbie."

"Back to the ranch? But won't the cops be waiting for you there."

"Probably. I was there last night to grab my lucky hat from the barn before I came to see you. I left a note for Robbie to stick around the house."

"Was that safe? Leaving the note I mean."

"Robbie knows I didn't hit poor old Nate over the head, and no-one else will understand what I wrote."

"That sounds intriguing," she said with a grin as he scooped up the last mouthful. "Would you like some more?"

"I'd love another helpin', but I'd better not."

Picking up their empty plates, she carried them to the sink, then grabbed the coffee pot, topped up his mug and sat back down.

"Now will you tell me your version of events?"

"Sure will. First, I swear I'd ended things with Patty just as I told you. We hadn't seen each other for a couple of months."

"Then why were you with her?"

"I'm getting to that. Before we broke up, she'd gotten real possessive, like, almost scary, and things were gettin' worse by the day. I knew I had to end things. She was upset, and I mean crazy upset, but as the weeks went by I thought things had settled down, then outta the blue she called. It was the afternoon of the night old man Nate got robbed."

"And you don't think it was a coincidence?"

"Not a chance," he said solemnly. "She said she needed to tell me something important, and it had to be in person. I said no initially, but she sounded sincere, so I agreed to meet her at the picnic grounds by the lake."

"Shit. That's just a couple of miles from the gas station."

"Yep! I drove up there, waited a good twenty minutes, and I was about to leave when she rolled up. All she did was accuse me of being a bastard, and said she'd never forgive me for ruinin' her life. That was it. I felt real bad, but she was gone before I even had a chance to calm her down. It made no sense at the time, none, but the next day the you-know-what hit the fan."

"But she claimed you contacted her, and when she met you, you wanted to have sex, and when she turned you down, you tried to force yourself on her."

"I swear to you Tess, on everything I hold dear, that was a bald-faced lie. I would never push a woman to have sex with me, but it was her word against mine, and everyone around here decided to believe her."

"Luke, I believe you, and forgive me for bringing this up, but they found the crowbar and money in your garage."

"Tess, think about it. How stupid would I be to hit poor old Nate, steal the money, and leave the evidence in my garage? I was totally set up. Someone stole my crowbar, used it on Nate, took his money, and left everything at my place where the police would find it. I have to assume the person responsible used Patty to help him."

"I'm so sorry I never gave you the chance to talk to me," she muttered, shaking her head. "Maybe I could have helped. Good grief. I feel so guilty."

"Tess," he said softly, reaching across the table and taking her hand, "it's okay. There was a lotta pressure on you, but now I'll be able to focus in on fixin' this mess."

"Lord, I hope so, but who would do this to you, and why?"

"You're not gonna like this."

"Tell me. I want to know so I can get my gun and shoot them."

"Tyler."

"Tyler? It can't be!"

"Because...?"

"Why would he risk everything to do something so despicable?"

"Hasn't he been after you since you were teenagers? Wasn't his family upset when you started goin' out with me, most especially him!"

"Well, yes, but—"

"Tess," Luke said, fixing her with a steady gaze, "there's no-one else. Until this happened, I was well-liked around here. Tyler is the only one who had an axe to grind, and Patty was angry enough to help him."

"How can we find out for sure? I'll do whatever it takes."

"Thanks, darlin'," he said softly, "but you've gotta start thinkin' like an alley cat."

"What does that mean?"

"Be ready for anything, and you can't let your emotions get the better of you. Can you do that?"

"I think so. I definitely need to play it cool with Jeb," she said with a sigh, recalling their earlier conversation. "I was really sharp with him this morning. He can be so patronizing."

"Like I said, you need a real good spankin'," Luke said, lowering his voice. "It would calm you down."

Tess felt the blood rush to her face, and though she dropped her eyes, she could feel him studying her.

"We need to get him off our backs," she mumbled, "certainly off mine."

"Yep, and I know how. Jeb needs to believe I'm somewhere else."

"That would work," she agreed enthusiastically, lifting her gaze, then reaching across the table, she traced her finger along the scar above his eye. "How did this happen?"

"I traded it for some teeth."

"Seems like you came out ahead," she quipped with a grin. "Teeth are important."

"It wasn't the easiest deal I ever made."

"Luke—all joking aside—I'm really glad you're back."

Taking her hand and lowering it from his forehead, he wrapped his fingers around hers.

"Me too, but I wasn't jokin' when I said you need a spankin'. You're nervous and on edge. We can't go into this thing with you all wired up, so I'm gonna take care of that right now. Go and change into a skirt, then wait for me."

CHAPTER THREE

HER BUTTERFLIES WILDLY fluttering, Tess moved quickly down the hall to her bedroom. Hastily making her bed and opening her closet, she stared at the skirts hanging in a neat row wondering which one to wear.

"Tess? Are you ready?"

Her heart skipped.

"One-second."

Hurriedly peeling off her jeans and grabbing the first skirt on the rack, she ran a brush through her hair, then turned and stared at the door.

"Okay. Come in."

Stepping into the room, he paused, then shook his head.

"What's wrong?" she asked anxiously. "Don't you like what I'm wearing?"

"I like it just fine, but damn, girl, you look terrified. This is just a spankin', not the firin' squad."

"I've never—uh—" she stammered, her face blazing red.

"Your daddy never spanked your butt?" he asked, raising his eyebrows. "That's surprising."

"Why?"

"Cos I'll bet you were a handful growin' up. Come to think of it, that's probably why you're a handful now."

"What do you mean?" she asked, her voice changing as her anxiety suddenly gave way to a streak of defiance.

"That right there," he replied with a chuckle. "You're difficult now 'cos you weren't taken in hand when you were a naughty little girl. I'll bet you had your daddy wrapped around your little finger."

She couldn't help but smile. It was an accusation she'd heard many times, especially from Jeb.

"Am I right?" Luke pressed. "Tell me the truth."

"Maybe," she admitted, and though her butterflies were still fluttering, she could feel herself beginning to settle down.

"And I bet he still is."

"Maybe," she said, the hint of a grin curling her lips.

"Uh-huh. Well, darlin', I may be crazy about you, but I'm still gonna spank your butt, I'll turn you over my knee whenever I think you need it."

"Did you have to say that?" she muttered, her anxiety returning with a vengeance. "You won't spank me hard will you?"

"Not this time, but I will in the future if you need it. Now you need to hear my rules, and they're written in stone."

"Rules? What kind of rules?"

"How hard I spank you and for how long, that's up to me," he declared, making her stomach churn as he parroted her earlier thoughts. "I'll listen to any defense you might offer, but if I think you need a real good spankin', you'll get it." Then pausing, he lowered his voice and added, "Tess, if that's not okay with you, tell me now before we take this thing between us any further. I'll walk out your door and I'll never bother you again."

A searing heat moved through her body, and her knees grew weak, forcing her to drop on the edge of the bed.

If I think you need a real good spankin', you'll get it...I'll walk out your door and I'll never bother you again.

His threats swirled through her head, but as much as his short speech unnerved her, she found him more compelling than ever.

"It is," she managed. "Okay with me, I mean."

Stepping forward and sitting next to her, he placed his arm around her shoulders and gave her a reassuring hug.

"Don't worry, darlin," he said softly. "This is just about calmin' you down. Punishin' you, that'll be different."

"Why would you have to punish me?"

"If and when that time comes, you'll find out. Now get yourself over my knee before I start thinkin' you're just stallin'. Trust me, you don't want that."

"I kind of am, and you can't blame me. This is weird."

"At least you're bein' honest! I'll tell you one more time, but after that, don't make me repeat myself. Crawl over my lap."

"This is so weird," she protested as she squirmed over his knees. "Oh, my God, I can't believe it."

"My other rules are simple," he declared, ignoring her outburst as he smoothed his hand over the skirt covering her upturned backside. "No throwin' your hands behind you. It's annoyin', and you don't wanna annoy me when I'm spankin' your butt. Got it?"

"Uh-huh."

"Lock your fingers together. That will remind you if you're tempted. Next rule, no yellin'. If you think you're gonna start makin' a bunch of noise, let me know and I'll grab you a pillow."

"You're scaring me."

"It's your first time, that's to be expected. Third and last rule, like I said before, I decide how hard I'm gonna spank you. Don't tell me to stop. If you do I'll add two hard swats. Do you understand the rules, Tess?"

"They're not difficult."

"It's a yes or no question," he retorted, his voice suddenly stern, "so now you need to repeat them."

"Um, I can't put my hands behind me, I, uh, I'm not allowed to yell, and you'll decided how long this will last."

"What happens if you tell me to stop?"

"You'll add two hard swats."

"Good. Time to begin."

"Oh, Lord, I—"

But abruptly lifting his hand and bringing it down with a sound slap, he cut her off before she could finish.

"Ow!"

"Don't be shoutin' out like that," he warned, squeezing where he'd spanked. "I won't remind you again."

"Sorry."

Landing the next smack, he repeated the squeeze. The third swat was harder, and so was his hard clasp. So it continued, and though she began to wriggle, he didn't stop the pattern. Smack, squeeze. Smack, squeeze, delivering his blows to the same spot time after time. The area began to burn with a hot sting.

"Luke, it hurts."

"Yep," he murmured, moving his hand to her opposite cheek. "Tess, do I have your attention?"

"Yes."

"I'm gonna spank you on this side, let you rest for a minute, then finish with a quick volley."

"It hurts."

"I heard you the first time, but you'll be a whole lot calmer when I'm done. If you get wired up and outta sorts again, you'll be right back here. Remember that when you start findin' yourself in a tizzy. It's about time you learned some self control," he finished, delivering the first slap.

Grasping her flesh for a second, he continued with the slow, rhythmic pace. Just when she was about to protest, he paused his hand.

"Thank God," she whimpered, letting out a breath.

"You got twenty good slaps on each side."

"If felt like a whole lot more," she declared, suddenly kicking out her feet.

"What was that?"

"I don't know. Just something I had to do."

He chuckled.

"I'm glad you find me amusing."

"Damn. Sassy even gettin' spanked," he remarked, pinching her quickly.

"Ouch!"

"You gonna behave?"

"I am behaving. I haven't put my hands behind me, I haven't yelled, and I haven't asked you to stop."

"That's followin' my rules, but that doesn't mean you're behavin'. You know very well you're testin' my patience. Did you forget I just told you there's more comin'?"

"Uh...sorry."

"I've gotta a feelin' you'll be doin' that a lot, but that's okay. Your ass, darlin'. I'm gonna pull your skirt up now, and don't worry. I'm not gonna bare your bottom, not this time."

She didn't protest.

He'd been right.

She'd wanted to test his resolve.

Now she had a feeling she'd pay the price.

But she'd needed to know.

Feeling the skirt slowly sliding across her thin panties, though fresh heat flared across her face, she couldn't deny the warm, needy dampness between her legs.

"This is gonna sting, but it'll be quick. Remember, no hands behind you, and no yellin'."

Gritting her teeth, she waited for the first blow, but he began fondling her, moving his hand across her sore bottom and down the back of her thighs. Sinking into his lap, relishing the divine caress, she prayed he'd slip his fingers against her hungry pussy.

But the blissful respite was fleeting.

A flurry of stinging smacks blasted across the fullness of her scalded backside. Squirming furiously, she stifled one, long, bleating whimper, but he stopped as quickly as he'd begun.

"Oh, my God!" she gasped, gyrating her hips in a twisting dance.

"Settle down, I'm done. You've had that comin' for a long time."

"I thought you said you wouldn't spank me hard."

"Darlin', that wasn't hard," he murmured, comforting her rough, smacked skin, "though I added to it because of your backtalk. Bear that in mind for the future."

"Ooh, I will. I swear."

"Sounds like someone's learned a lesson."

"I have. Shit."

"Quit your cussin', and take a deep breath. Relax, Tess, focus on my hand rubbin' away the sting."

Sucking in the air, she closed her eyes, but as she surrendered, she felt her thighs tighten as a deep carnal need moved through her body.

Silent minutes ticked by.

"Come on," he finally murmured. "Time to get up."

Helping her off his lap and on to the bed, he stretched out next to her and pulled her into his muscled arms.

Melting against him, she couldn't hold back.

"Luke?"

"Yeah, darlin'?"

"Please will you kiss me."

"There's nothin' in this world I want more than to kiss you," he said softly, "but if I do, I won't stop there."

"I don't want you to."

"Are you sure?"

"Totally, completely, one-hundred percent sure."

In an instant his lips were on hers in a soft, delicious, lingering kiss, but his mouth grew demanding. Their fervent passion took hold. Quickly removing her clothes, he paused to gaze at her nakedness.

"Damn, Tess, you're so beautiful."

"I need you," she mewled, raising her arms. "Please, Luke, I need you so badly."

Hurriedly pulling off his robe, he lowered his mouth to her breasts, sucking hungrily and kneading her full, fleshy mounds.

"I've dreamed about this so many times," she breathed. "All the time you were away I thought about you being in my bed. It's true...all the time..."

"Me too, darlin'," he muttered, kissing his way down her body.

Dropping his head between her legs, he lapped her pussy, evoking a sharp gasp, then a cry as he roughly grabbed her spanked cheeks and raised her hips. But she fell into an endless moan as his mouth devoured her, and his tongue twirled around her clit in an endless, torturous dance. Just as she was about to erupt, he slid up the length of her body, placed his rigid cock against her slick wetness, and plunged himself home.

As he pumped with slow, strong, deliberate thrusts, his hands roamed over her body, exploring every inch as he nipped her nipples and bit her neck—but his fever took hold. Unable to maintain the measured pace, he accelerated, pounding her pussy and quickly reaching the brink.

"Let go, Tess, come with me."

Giving herself up to the sparkling orgasm, sure she would shatter into a thousand pieces, she let out a deep moan, but he dropped his mouth over hers, muffling their mutual groans. Wave after glorious wave swept them away, until the last convulsion rippled into nothingness.

Breathless and drained, he collapsed at her side, and falling limp, her body still tingling, she sank against his chest. His heart pounded against her ear, and in spite of the danger, she couldn't remember ever feeling so happy and at peace.

"We have to fix things," she finally murmured, moving her fingertips across his wiry chest hair. "You have to be cleared so we can be together."

"Keep the faith. It will work out," he promised, then rolling on his side, he smiled down at her. "Did that calm you down?"

"Are you kidding?" she replied with a giggle.

"I was talking about your hot ass."

"Oh, that."

"Sassy girl."

"Honestly, I hate to admit it, but yeah. It worked better than a massage. Way better."

"Now you'll be able to deal with your brother and not lose your temper."

"I think you might be right, but where do we go from here?"

"Not *we* darlin'. I know what has to be done, but I'm not lettin' you risk your neck."

"But I want to help, I mean, really help."

"There is one thing you might be able to do for me. By any chance do you have men's shirts or jeans here?"

"I do!" she exclaimed. "Dad gave me a box for the church sale next month. There might be something in there. I also have a jacket I layer sweaters under. That might fit."

"Great. Anything would be better than what I've been trapped in these last few days."

"What else?"

"Mostly you can help by staying safe and doin' what you're told. I know you're a tough, determined woman, but remember, I'm a wanted man. It's bad enough you're harborin' a fugitive."

"I'm helping an innocent man find justice!"

"Be that as it may, it's still illegal."

"There must be something I can do."

He paused.

"What?" she pressed. "Oh, my gosh, there is something."

"Yep. I'm just not sure if I'm gonna let you do it."

CHAPTER FOUR

SITTING AT THE KITCHEN table and drinking piping hot, fresh mugs of coffee, Luke explained the details of his plan, then told Tess the part she could play. But he remained worried.

"If something goes wrong and I'm captured it won't take them long to figure out how you helped me, and maybe even worse, you might get caught in the act!"

"You don't have to worry about that," she retorted. "There are no security cameras around here, and I told you how it will be easy for me to do the job, but if I'm going to pull it off I have to go now. The manager will be leaving for lunch shortly."

"I'm still not crazy about this."

"Well you can't do it," she said pointedly, "so what choice do we have? That box of dad's clothes is in the closet in the guest room. While you're sorting through it, I'll run the errand."

"Dammit..." he muttered under his breath. "I wish I could think of another way."

"There isn't one. Stop worrying. I'll be back before you know it."

"Of course I'm gonna worry," he declared, "but you're right. There's no other way. Now, Tess, if there's even the whiff of a problem, don't do it. You hear me?"

"Yes, Mr. Bossman, I hear you," she said with a sassy grin.

"I'm serious! Do I need to tan your tail again?"

"No! I don't have any desire to get caught. I swear I'll be super cautious, but please can I go now?"

"I guess you'd better," he said reluctantly.

"Thank you!"

Jumping to her feet, she stepped around the table and planted a quick kiss on his cheek.

"I'm outta here!"

"Make sure you're not followed, and be quick. Don't stand around gossiping," he said firmly, then pushing back from the table and abruptly grabbing her waist, he yanked her into his body. "I love you, Tess Turner. Don't you forget it. You be real, real careful."

"I will, and thank you for letting me do this. I feel so bad about what happened. I want to make it up to you."

"Hey, I'm the one who's grateful, darlin', and you've got nothin' to be sorry about. Now go on, before I change my mind."

Watching her happily hurry away, he sat back down, picked up his coffee, and pondered his plan. Finally satisfied he hadn't missed anything, he headed down the hall to the guest room.

In addition to the box, he found a decent-sized, empty backpack. Carrying both and placing them on the bed, he began rummaging through the clothes. Finding plenty from which to choose, he gratefully dressed in a warm, fuzzy, pendelton shirt and thick, black denim jeans, then stuffed another pair into the bag, along with a heavy, grey wool sweater, and a charcoal grey sports jacket.

"Wow, they fit great," Tess declared, entering the room.

"You're back!" he exclaimed. "I didn't hear the car. How did it go?"

"I'm here and smiling, aren't I?"

Opening her hobo bag, she pulled out three phones she'd whisked from the shelf at the local drugstore.

"Even though it always takes Amanda a few minutes to find my special order energy bars from the back, my heart was pounding when I slipped these into my bag. I've never stolen anything in my life."

"That's why you were able to get away with it," he said with a grin. "Everyone in this town knows how honest you are. Even if someone had watched you put them in your bag, they would have thought you'd already paid for them, or would have before leaving. Speaking of which, were there other people in the store?"

"Just a couple of teenagers, and they were engrossed in the makeup department. It was still nerve-racking though. I was trembling when I walked out of there."

"Soon I'll be able to make you tremble in a good way," he murmured.

Taking the bag from her hands and dropping it on the bed, he slid his fingers into her hair, clutched it tightly, and pressed his lips fervently against hers. "Dammit, now I wanna ravage you again right now."

"You won't get any objection from me," she whispered, melting against him.

"I don't have time, darlin', but I will soon, and that's a promise. We need to trade numbers so I can get moving. I'm running out of time."

"You know how to activate them?"

"One of the many talents I picked up in prison."

Ripping open the packages, he tinkered with them for a few minutes, then making sure the numbers worked, he handed her one, put another in his pocket, and packed the third in the backpack.

"I'll talk to you soon," he murmured, pulling her into his arms. "I can't thank you enough for doing all this."

"I'm still so sorry about—"

"Shush. That's ancient history."

"I still don't know how you're going to pull this off. All it will take is one small thing to go wrong and you'll be toast. Please let me come along. I can run interference, maybe cause a distraction if you need one."

"Tess, the next few days will be risky, and that's why you need to stay here."

"I'll do my best, but it won't be easy."

"Not good enough," he said, dropping his voice and fixing her with a steely gaze. "I can't worry about you. I'll be busy enough stayin' one step ahead of everyone else."

"Okay, okay, I'll stay here," she promised, but covertly moved her hands behind her back and crossed her fingers.

"You know what time to make the call."

"Yes, Luke, absolutely."

"Then I guess I'll get movin'."

Picking up the backpack and grabbing his lucky hat he smiled down at her.

"Keep the faith, and don't forget, I'm a crafty fella," he said with a chuckle.

"I have some freshly baked muffins. You should take a couple."

"I won't say no to that!"

Following her down the hall and into the kitchen, he munched on one as she wrapped two more in cling fill and placed them in the outside pocket of the rucksack.

"There. At least you won't totally starve. Shoot, I could have made you sandwiches and—"

"I'll be fine," he murmured, leaning down and kissing her softly.

"Please call me when you can?"

"Of course I will."

Unable to stop himself, he pressed his mouth on hers one last them, then moved quickly out the back door.

AT THE SHERIFF'S OFFICE, Jeb had his feet kicked up on his desk, and was staring at the freshly printed wanted poster featuring Luke Larson.

"Don't worry, Jeb, we'll catch him."

Looking up Jeb saw the tired face of Dwayne Johnson. The young deputy had been on patrol all night.

"Sure we will," Jeb said, dropping his feet back on the floor and sitting up. "He and my sister were nuts about each other. He won't be able to resist tryin' to see her, but what are you doin' here? You should be home sleepin'."

"I grabbed a cat nap in the lounge, but I can go back tonight if you want," Dwayne said eagerly. "I wasn't bored, not at all. I liked it. I don't know why the fellas complain about stakeouts."

"You go on home, Dwayne. If I need you I'll call you."

"Okay, Jeb, but I wanna keep workin', I really do. I wanna prove myself."

"That's good, Dwayne, but you'll be no use to anyone if you're too tired. You can't keep watch if you're fallin' asleep. You think you're fine, then it creep up. Believe me, I know what I'm talkin' about."

"Oh, yeah, I guess that could happen. I'll see you later then."

Watching him amble away, Jeb let out a sigh. He liked Dwayne. The kid was solid and had a big heart, but in spite of his uncle's determination to make a cop out of him, Jeb knew it was like trying to teach someone with two left feet how to dance. It didn't help that Dwayne had no desire to be in law enforcement. Jeb had taken him out for a beer one night, and the young deputy had told him what he really wanted to do was work at the animal shelter.

"I love critters," he'd said, a faraway look in his eyes. "I want to become an Animal Control Officer and rescue all the poor strays. I'd adopt every last one of them if I had the land and the money."

Jeb could see it. Dwayne was like a big puppy himself.

"Maybe Tess was right," Jeb muttered. "That kid wouldn't stand a chance if he ran into Larson—assuming he was the one who hit old man Nate on the head."

A frown crossing his forehead, Jeb looked back at the poster. In spite of what he'd said to Tess, and accepting the sheriff's determination that Luke was the guilty party, over the months that had passed Jeb had started to have doubts. Luke Larson had always struck him as the kind of guy who'd step up to rescue an old man, not smash him over the head with a crowbar. But now Luke had escaped, and it was Jeb's job to find him and bring him in.

"That's what I'm gonna do," he grunted, "and I'll move heaven and earth to protect my sister."

The ringing of his cell phone broke into his thoughts. Seeing Tess's name on the screen he answered the call.

"Speak of the devil," he muttered. "Hey, Tess. I was just thinkin' about you."

"Jeb, I just heard from him," she declared breathlessly. "Luke! I just heard from Luke."

"Seriously? Luke Larson called you?" Jeb asked, almost shouting as he jumped to his feet. "What'd he say?"

Several other deputies in earshot moved quickly across to Jeb's desk to listen, including Dwayne, who still hadn't left the station.

"He wanted to see me but I told him absolutely not," Tess exclaimed. "He pleaded his case for a while then finally gave up, but, Jeb, he said he'd be heading out of town right away."

"Did he say where he was going or how he was leaving?" Jeb asked urgently. "Did he give you any clue at all?"

"No, but a thought has crossed my mind."

"Tell me quickly, Tess," Jeb demanded, grabbing a pen and searching for a piece of paper.

"There's the daily nonstop to Longville that leaves at 1 p.m. If he hopped on that train he'd be miles away fast, and with no-one getting on or off for a couple of hours he be able to relax. He sounded exhausted. If I was him that's what I'd do."

"Tess, you're a genius," Jeb pronounced, then staring up at the clock on the wall he saw it was almost 12:45. "I've gotta go, but I'll keep you posted."

"Larson's been spotted?" one of the deputies asked as Jeb ended the call.

"Yep, and he could be on that speed train headin' up to Longville, but we've gotta move fast. Listen up!"

Quickly selecting the deputies he wanted with him, he sent others to patrol the streets Luke would probably take to reach the station. Seeing Dwayne's disappointed face, Jeb asked him to stake out Luke's ranch.

"He could just as easily go there," Jeb said solemnly, though he didn't believe it for a minute. "I know you're off duty, but if you wouldn't mind sittin' in your own car over there, that'd be a big help. If you see him, or notice anything out of the ordinary, call me."

"Sure, I'd be happy to," Dwayne said eagerly. "Thanks, Jeb."

Dwayne's delighted expression told Jeb he'd done the right thing. The kid would be out of harm's way, and feel like part of the team.

BACK AT THE HOUSE AND hearing a siren, she ran into her lounge and peered out the front window. A patrol car sped past and squealed around the corner at the end of the block.

"Keystone cops," she said with a giggle. "Luke, you really are a crafty fella." Letting the curtain fall, she headed into the guest room to straighten up, but as she wiped down the bathroom counter, she began obsessing about Luke's safety.

"I should go to the cafe early," she muttered. "I can't hang around here for two hours. I'll lose my mind."

Picking up the towel he'd used and clothes he'd been wearing, she carried them into the laundry, threw them in the washing machine, and started it up.

"Yes, that's exactly what I'll do," she said decisively. "I can start the lamb stew. It will be even better if it simmers for an extra hour."

But even as she brushed her hair and put on her makeup she knew she was lying to herself.

She had no intention of going into work.

Walking into the garage and backing out on to the street, she turned the car in the direction of the railway station.

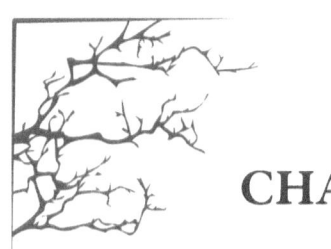

CHAPTER FIVE

RARELY DID JEB SWEAR, especially in public, but the fury burning through him could not be controlled. The ticket seller had confirmed Luke Larson had bought a fare on the nonstop train, and Jeb had missed the train's departure by only a few minutes. Marching up and down the platform, he cursed under his breath.

"Fuck!" he growled, his fingers curling into clenched fists. "A few fucking minutes! I could've had him! I could have fucking had him."

Jeb's closest friend, Alex Brewster, a deputy with ambitions of becoming a detective, kept pace, trying to settle him down.

"But, Jeb, this is good news. Now we know where Larson is and where he's going. We can radio ahead and have the boys in Longville pick him up."

"Dammit, Alex, I wanna be the one to bring him in."

"Then jump in your car and go after him. You might just make it."

Suddenly stopping, Jeb threw his arms in the air.

"Alex! It's a non-stop! How the hell can I beat it?"

"Even if you don't you'll still find him. Longville's a small town. Get a grip, Jeb. You're wastin' time."

Letting out a heavy breath, Jeb stared at his friend.

"You're right, dammit. Thanks, Alex. You wanna join me?"

"I'm gonna stick around here. You and Sam will get the job done. He's probably leanin' against your car waitin' for you to see sense and join him."

"Yeah. If you can't be my partner, I can't do better than Sam. I'm outta here."

Jeb jogged off, but Alex paused to stare around the empty platform.

An odd feeling moved through his stomach.

Returning to the small station house, he wandered up to the ticket counter, leaned his elbows on the shelf, and smiled at the elderly gent behind the glass.

"Hey, Miles."

"Hey, Deputy. Sorry you missed him."

"Are you sure it was Luke Larson who bought the ticket?"

"It was Luke Larson all right," the old man replied, fervently nodding his head. "That's why I called. I never knew the boy, but Nate's a friend of mine and I was real upset about what happened. What kinda fella hits an old man? It was a bad business, and I was shook up when Larson walked up to this counter. I was scared. I was real scared."

"I'm sure you were," Alex said patiently. "Did you see him actually board the train?"

"Yep, right there, plain as day," the old man declared, pointing towards the platform.

"Did you walk out and watch the train leave?"

"Sure did. I always do."

"Did you see anyone who looked out of place, or anything out of the ordinary?"

"Well, let me see, there was a fella in a suit, not a full suit. He was wearin' a suit jacket with jeans. You know the young folk do that these days. Makes no sense to me. Do you mix the dressy stuff with the regular?"

"Not too much," Alex answered with a grin. "Where did this fella go?"

"Walked off the end of the platform near where the woods start. I didn't see where he went from there."

"Okay, thanks for you help."

"Any time. We can't have nasty men like Luke Larson runnin' around free. I sure hope you catch him quick."

"I'm sure we will, sir."

But stepping away, Alex was convinced Luke hadn't boarded the train, or if he had, he'd slipped off before it left the station. He wasn't a stupid man, certainly not stupid enough to show his well-known face, then board a train he'd be forced to stay on for two hours.

"No," Alex muttered. "He would've been on a train with plenty of stops so he could get off along the way."

Walking back to the platform, Alex stared across at the thicket.

PARKED UNDER THE SHADOW of a tree in front of the station, Tess had been watching the activity on the far side of the parking lot. As the patrol cars began to leave, and her brother burned rubber as he'd sped away, she'd smiled broadly and sighed with relief. Luke's plan had worked. Starting up her car and driving to the exit, she stopped to wait for traffic.

Her smiled vanished.

A squad car sat parked on the street.

Quickly turning around and driving back into the parking area, she climbed from her car and raced through the station house to the empty platform. Squinting as she stared towards the woods, she spotted a deputy disappearing into the trees.

"Oh, no, this is a nightmare," she exclaimed. "I have to find you before he does!"

Her heart racing, she dashed back to her car.

Luke's plan had been simple.

Buy the ticket and board, change clothes in the toilet, duck out of the train seconds before it left and head into the woods.

"Your brother will take off on a wild goose chase, and the rest of the deputies will be back to work as usual," Luke had said.

"But all it will take is one small thing to go wrong and you'll be toast," she'd replied.

"I was right," she mumbled under her breath, climbing back into her car. "Darn it, Luke!"

Putting her foot down, she raced to the entrance of the small forest, parked on the rough edge, then hurriedly climbed from her car and entered the thicket. Though she tried to walk quietly, it wasn't easy. Dried leaves and dead branches crunched beneath her feet. Darting her eyes from side to side, searching for both Luke and the deputy, a flash of movement made her stop. Ducking down, she peered through the foliage.

A tall, burly frame in uniform came into view.

Alex Brewster!

The brawny deputy had asked her out, but growing up with a brother in the force she knew how tough it was being involved with a cop. Though she genuinely liked Alex, she'd turned him down. Watching him move stealthily through the trees she realized he was heading east. Luke would be heading west to his ranch. Feeling a wave of relief, she veered off and quickened her pace.

But the woods could be deceptive.

Not wanting to get lost, she paused to make a mental note of where she was relative to where she'd entered, noting landmarks she could use to make her way back to the car.

"Satellites orbit the planet and talk to NASA, but I can't get cell service."

The deep male voice was unmistakably Luke's.

Moving through a thick clump of young saplings, she spotted him holding his phone high in the air searching for a signal.

"Luke," she said with hushed urgency as she burst through the brush. "Keep your voice down."

SPINNING AROUND, LUKE stared at Tess in disbelief. With both anger and joy flooding his heart, he was about to demand an explanation, but she brought her finger to her mouth and rushed up to him.

"Alex Brewster is here," she whispered, pointing in the direction she'd last seen the deputy. "He's only about a hundred yards away."

Lifting his gaze, Luke saw movement in the distance.

"Come with me," he breathed, grabbing her hand.

Leading her back through the thicket to a large, fallen tree trunk, they stretched out on their stomachs and peered over the top.

"You'd better have a good explanation for being here," he murmured, his eyes scanning his surroundings.

"Please don't be mad. I do. I saw—"

But a rush of excited birds flew from the treetops, startling them both.

Tess dropped her head down, but Luke had spotted the deputy.

The man resembled a bear.

Moving in a slow circle, he stared into the woods, his chin tilted up as if sniffing the air.

Carefully picking up a large stone, Luke held his breath and waited.

The deputy finally turned his back to them.

His pulse racing, Luke rose to his feet, and praying he wouldn't hit a tree, he hurled the rock into the forest. Hastily dropping back down, he watched the cop freeze, then dart through the trees in the direction of the sound. In less than a minute he'd disappeared.

"Dammit, Tess," he said quietly, standing up and helping her to her feet, "I don't know whether to scold you and promise you the spankin' of your life, or hug you like crazy."

"A hug would be g-good," she stammered. "I've never been so scared."

Wrapping her into his arms and holding her tightly, he wondered how they'd escaped such a close call, then breaking away, he stepped back and stared at the ground.

"Did you lose something, and where's your lucky hat?"

"Nope, this here's what I'm looking for," he replied picking a long, thin stick, "and my hat's unhappily scrunched up in the backpack. I'll put it on once I'm outta the woods."

"What's the stick for?"

He paused.

"I was about to blast it against your backside, but I'd better wait. I don't want you yellin' and bringin' that deputy back here."

"But, Luke, I needed to warn you."

"We'll talk about this later. Get back to your car and go home. I'll call you when I make it to the ranch. It'll probably take me about an hour, maybe less, just depends."

"Okay, I'm going, but please be careful."

"Tess," he said, softening his voice, "I know you're worried, but this will all work out. I am gonna whip your butt though, just as soon as I can."

"But if I hadn't—"

"Hush up, or do you want me to change my mind and deal with you right now?"

"No! You have to go. Alex might come back this way."

"Then quit arguin'! Now where's your car?"

"Um, it's parked on the dirt road at the entrance to the forest."

"I know a short cut."

Keeping a watchful eye out for Alex, she followed Luke through the trees, and though she knew he was upset with her, she had no regrets.

"There's your car," he said quietly, pointing ahead. "Drive straight home, you hear me?"

"I will, but please be careful, Luke."

"I know what I'm doin', Tess. You've gotta trust me."

"Won't you please tell me where you'll be hiding out? What if there's an emergency? What if I need to reach you?"

"It's safer if you don't know, darlin'—for both of us, and you've got the phone."

"Oh, right," she said sheepishly. "But what if you can't answer?"

"Tess," he said sharply, "like I said, you've gotta trust me."

"Sorry."

"It's okay. Now I need to take off before that deputy decides to come this way," he murmured. "You behave!"

"No promises," she replied with a wink.

Grinning back at her and kissing her softly, he gave her a reassuring smile, then turned and marched away.

Walking to her car and climbing behind the wheel, she watched him head towards the steep bank that would take him away from the woods, but her mind wouldn't let her rest. She knew he'd be skirting the river bed for a couple of miles, then hiking over some small hills and down to his ranch.

"I can't let you go without any kind of backup," she muttered, a worried frown creasing her forehead. "I'm sorry, Luke, but I can't. I'll follow you from a safe distance for a few minutes, and if Alex shows up I'll be able to distract him. You'll never know, and I'll be able to sleep tonight."

Turning off her car and climbing out, she pretended not to hear the warning voice in her head, the one that said she was being reckless, and she was in enough trouble already.

It was like a vague shadow on a cloudy day.

Happy with her decision, she started jogging to the spot she'd just left him. She and her friends used to play by river as children. She knew the area well, and she was sure she'd have no trouble staying hidden as she dogged his steps, but she had to hurry. He'd be walking at a fast clip, and if she was going to catch up and keep him in sight, she needed to pick up her pace.

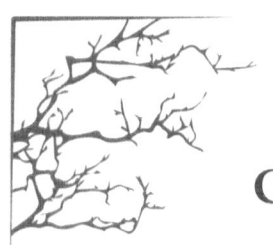

CHAPTER SIX

IN SPITE OF THE DANGER he faced, Luke felt nothing but exhilaration hiking to his ranch. Finding himself surrounded by the gentle slopes and patches of trees scattered across the fields was almost surreal. There had been a light dusting of snow the night before, but the sun was shining, offering its warm comfort to the chilly day. He'd always seen his land as God's country, and he could hear Blake Shelton's hit echoing through his head.

Though he'd almost given in when Tess had begged to know where he'd be hiding out, he'd managed to hold his resolve, though a part of him wished he'd told her. He would have liked nothing better than having her alone and at his mercy at the isolated refuge. He smiled as he pictured it. No-one would think to look for him there.

Tyler Anderson lived on his father's property in a large cabin close to the main house. It was a sprawling ranch adjacent to Tess's family home. Luke had decided the only way to expose Tyler was to watch him, maybe even break into his house to search for a clue that might help to prove his guilt.

There were several cabins scattered across the hundreds of acres owned by the Andersons, one of which served as a seasonal hunting lodge. The luxurious three bedroom home came complete with satellite television, central heating and air-conditioning, and offered a six horse, insulated barn.

The first week in October the lodge was locked up for the winter months, then reopened the last week in April. Nestled in a cluster of small knolls and surrounded by trees, it couldn't be seen from the grand home or the other cottages. The unique location offered visitors a sense of living in the great outdoors, while being conveniently close to the main house and its driveway back to the road.

Luke had been just twelve years old when he'd started working there, caring for the horses and running errands. Home for the summer during his college years, he'd lead the guests on long trail rides, some lasting several hours.

With his deep knowledge of the surrounding area, staying at the lodge would give him an advantage if he was discovered, and just as importantly, Tyler's cabin was just a short distance away. Luke couldn't think of a more comfortable or convenient place in which to hide.

But as he neared his home, he shifted his focus, his eyes darting from side to side watching for any movement. Climbing over the fence, he dropped into the field that would take him to the back of his property. He needed to collect Ghost, his white quarter horse, for the ride to the hunting lodge.

PARKED UNDER A GROUP of trees on top of a small knoll a few hundred feet from Luke's house, Dwayne yawned and shifted in his seat. Though the view wasn't a particularly good one, he was concerned about being spotted if he stopped any closer. He'd been in position for over an hour when Deputy Brewster had called. It was suspected Luke Larson had hopped a train and was headed to Longville.

"Jeb's chasing him, but you should stay where you are," Alex had declared. "There's no telling with Luke Larson. He's a wily one."

"That's what everyone keeps saying," Dwayne had remarked. "Don't worry, I'll keep a close look out."

Even though he was dog-tired, Dwayne didn't mind a bit. Alex Brewster was a cop with keen instincts who thought it was a good idea for him to stay there. Dwayne was happy—almost excited—by Alex's faith in him. But in spite of his desire to be conscientious, Dwayne was bleary-eyed and growing more tired by the minute.

Suddenly spotting a lone figure hiking towards the barn from the back fields, his bloodshot eyes popped wide. Lifting his binoculars, he peered into the distance, but all he could make out was the man putting one foot in front of the other, and his black cowboy hat standing out against the thin layer of white snow on the ground. Deciding to walk down the bank to get a better look, Dwayne climbed from his car and started down the gentle slope, completely forgetting his cell phone resting in its holder on the center console.

Moving slowly, worried about slipping on the slick ground, by the time he reached level ground, the man was inside the barn. Creeping forward, he approached the open door...

THRILLED TO SEE HIS boss, Robbie threw his macho pride out the window, hugging Luke with gusto as he fought back tears of relief and joy.

"Man it's good to see you," Robbie exclaimed. "I've been doin' my best to keep things goin' around here, but this place can't run right without you."

"I'm gonna sort all this out," Luke promised as he broke away from the brawny ranch hand. "I don't know how long it's gonna take, but I will. Did you understand the note?"

"I sure did," Robbie replied with a wide grin. "When I saw that piece of paper where your hat had been sittin', I damn near had a heart attack. The saddle bags are all set, socks and underwear in one, jeans and a couple of shirts in the other. I'm dyin' to hear where you'll be campin' out."

"The summer hunting lodge on the Anderson property," Luke replied. "No one can get there this time of year except by horse, and why would they bother?"

"Hey, boss, that's genius. I can bring you up some supplies tonight if you want."

"I have a phone for you, so I'll check what's there and let you know. They usually keep the freezer stocked, and there's always plenty of canned goods in the pantry. Hay shouldn't be a problem either. There's always plenty left over, and grain in sealed containers in the feed room, so Ghost will be fine too."

"I shoulda known you'd have this all figured out. There ain't nobody can plan like you, except maybe the people who set you up."

"At the time I was sure the cops would find the bastard," Luke said solemnly. "I thought it would be obvious someone had stashed the crowbar and stolen cash in my garage, but apparently they couldn't see the forest for the trees. How stupid would I have been to leave it there? What happened to common sense and thinkin' things through before rushin' to judgement. So much for justice."

"Yeah, that was a bad time," Robbie muttered. "Everyone knows you're a stand up guy."

"Bein' found guilty of attackin' poor Nate has been real hard. I love that old guy, but I've had plenty of time to think about the whole sorry mess and I've figured it out."

"You mean—you know who screwed you over?"

"Yep, but it's not gonna be easy to prove."

"I'll do whatever I can to help," Robbie offered earnestly. "Just tell me, anything at all."

"Thanks, Robbie. You know I'm a law-abidin' citizen, and I won't ask you to do anything illegal...though I guess helpin' me you already are."

"I don't care. It's a disgrace, what's happened, an absolute disgrace."

"It sure is, and thanks for your loyalty, Robbie. It means more than I can say, but I'd best get movin'. Here's your burner phone," he continued, reaching into his backpack. "My number's already stored. Tess Turner has one too. You can trust her."

"Is that right?" Robbie remarked raising his eyebrows. "I don't know how you managed it, but I'm sure glad you did."

"But she doesn't know I'll be at the lodge and I need to keep it that way, for her own sake as well as mine! Knowin' her, she'll decide to pop in for a visit, and I have to keep her safe. The last thing I want is her gettin' in trouble with the law."

"Hey, that makes all the sense in the world, especially with the Deputy Sheriff bein' her brother an' all."

"Now that I think about it, I'd better call you when I get there. If you don't hear from me in say, ninety minutes, come lookin'. It means I've either run into a problem on the way, or I've been picked up, though that probably won't happen. They think I'm on a train to Longville."

"No shit? How'd you manage that?"

"I'll tell you over a beer when all this is behind us, and the culprit who pulled this crap is the one behind bars."

"When you find the proof on that dirtbag, I'll shoot him myself."

"Please don't," Luke said with a chuckle. "You'll end up in the slammer, and I'll have to run this place without you."

"Good point!"

"Where's Ghost? Did you bring him in from pasture?"

"I never took him out," Robbie replied. "I had an inklin' you might find a way to get back here, and I wanted him nearby just in case. He's been livin' in the big corral with Chester, Blue and Skeeter. I'll go get him. I know he's been missin' you. He moped around for the first couple of months you were gone. I gave him extra attention, and bein' with his buddies probably helped."

"I sure have missed him," Luke said with a sigh. "I missed everything. I'm gonna clear my name. I have to."

STANDING JUST SHY OF the doorway, Dwayne was shocked by what he'd heard. Luke Larson was an innocent man, but Robbie was suddenly marching towards the door. Ducking away, Dwayne trudged up the knoll to his car. Out of breath by the time he reached it, he climbed inside, panting as he gazed down at the barn and the house beyond. If he turned in a wanted fugitive, he'd be a hero.

"But this is wrong," he muttered, a deep frown carving his forehead. "They'll just throw him back in prison, and he's innocent. Dammit. What the hell should I do?"

A deep frown carving his forehead, he started his car and headed to the main highway. He needed a beer and a long think.

OUT OF SIGHT IN A SMALL thicket, Tess sat uncomfortably on a stump watching the barn. She'd seen Luke disappear inside, and a few minutes later, Robbie, his ranch hand, had emerged. Though it had felt good to catch her breath, her bottom still carried a prickling soreness from Luke's hard, spanking hand, but the memory of the morning brought a soft smile to her lips. Closing her eyes, she relived the idyllic time she'd spent with him.

"I was crazy about you before," she whispered, recalling how marvelous she had felt being wrapped up in his muscled arms, "but now we've been together— truly together—I know I love you with all my heart, and I always have. How could I have been so stupid?"

Slowly opening her eyes and scanning the terrain, there appeared to be nothing for miles. She couldn't imagine where Luke would be heading when he left his ranch. Not knowing made it difficult to decide whether to continue to follow him, or head back to the railway station, pick up her car and go home. But the thought of leaving before knowing he was securely hidden away was too much to bear.

"Once you're settled and safe, I'll go," she said decisively, "but I have to know where you are."

Standing up to stretch, she stared down at the barn.

Her heart skipped.

Wearing his telltale black cowboy hat, Luke was riding a hefty white horse towards the hills skirting his property. Though the animal was only walking, he was moving at a fast clip.

Panicking, she broke into a jog.

She knew it was a bad idea, but she couldn't stop herself.

She had to know where he'd be hiding.

She just had to.

CHAPTER SEVEN

RIDING IN THE CLEAN air and across the open spaces had calmed Luke's troubled soul. Ghost had also expressed his joy, occasionally jigging and tossing his head from sheer happiness. The journey to the lodge had taken almost an hour, and with the sun slipping behind the distant mountain range, the temperature was falling rapidly. Navigating his way down the gentle slope to the lodge, Luke brought Ghost to a stop outside the barn, but climbing from the saddle he thought he heard the sound of an animal in distress. As Ghost pricked his ears and jerked his head around, Luke followed his horse's gaze. Staring up the hill Luke spotted an oddly shaped lump lying on the ground.

"I'll take care of you first, buddy," he said softly, patting Ghost on the neck.

Opening the barn door and leading his horse inside, Luke removed the saddle and bridle, guided him into the roomiest stall, then entered the tack room he knew so well. Nothing had changed. Taking what he needed, he returned to Ghost and brushed him off. Loving the attention, his horse nickered gratefully.

"Did you miss me, fella?" Luke purred. "I've missed you too, a whole lot."

Being alone with the big gelding in the quiet, empty barn was the perfect end to the exhilarating yet relaxing ride, and in spite of the heavy burden he carried, Luke felt at peace.

"Don't you worry Ghost, things will get back to normal," he promised, believing the words as he spoke them. "It will just take a little time."

Filling the water bucket, then dropping two flakes of hay into the large stall, he grabbed the saddle bags and headed outside. The air carried an icy nip, and with twilight fading he'd soon be faced with a dark sky. Dropping the saddle bags at the front door, he zipped up his lambswool, suede jacket, and made his way as quickly as he could up the slope. An injured animal could be dangerous, and drawing near, Luke paused.

The creature moved, then groaned.

"Damn, you're no animal."

Charging forward and crouching next to the crumpled body lying face down in the snow, he tentatively touched a shoulder.

"Hey, can you hear me?"

"Uh-huh..."

Luke caught his breath.

It was Tess.

"Are you in pain?" he asked, trying to come to grips with finding her.

"M-my ankle and m-my h-head," she stammered, turning to gaze up at him. He grimaced as he spied a nasty gash on her forehead, and hastily pulling off his jacket, he gently helped her sit up and he wrapped it around her.

"Luke, thank God you found me," she whimpered. "I'm so dizzy and c-cold."

"You'll be fine," he said, trying to sound reassuring as he scooped her up. "That's a bad cut on your head. That's probably why you're lightheaded."

"I f-fell, and I'm f-freezing."

"I know, darlin'. Don't worry, I'll get you inside and warm you up real quick."

As worried as he was angry, he scooped her up and made his way carefully down the hill. Reaching the covered verandah, he sat her on an old wooden trunk used to hold firewood, then fished around the back of the overhead light. To his great relief he found the key in its usual hiding place.

Quickly opening the door, he picked her up and carried her inside, laying her on the large, leather couch that had been in the lodge for as long as he could remember. Returning to the porch and grabbing the saddle bags, he closed and locked the door behind him, turned on the heat, then hurried to the hall closet, hoping it was where they still kept the medicine box and extra blankets. He found them both.

"I'm so glad Anderson hates change," he mumbled, striding back to her. "Don't worry, Tess, I'm gonna take care of you."

"I'm sorry, Luke," she bleated woefully. "I just wanted to make sure you were okay. I didn't know you'd be going so far."

"Shush," he said, covering her with a thick wool throw. "I need to dress this cut, but it's gonna sting," he warned, thinking her ass would be stinging even more as soon as she recovered.

Pouring the iodine solution on the gauze and gently cleaning the wound, he discovered the gash wasn't as deep as he'd initially thought. Placing a sterile patch over the cut, he taped it in place, then turned his attention to her ankle.

"I'm gonna have to take off your boots," Luke said gravely, staring up at her. "I'll be as gentle as I can."

"Okay. Uh, I really am sorry."

"I'm sure you are," he said with a sigh. "How did you hit your head?"

"You were getting ahead of me, and I was so focused on keeping you in sight I didn't see the edge of a low branch. It almost knocked me out. It hurt so much," she sniffled as tears brimmed in her eyes. "When I got up you were gone. I could follow your trail, but I was scared so I started to run. I thought I was going to faint I was panting so much, but I finally caught sight of you. I guess you'd stopped to look at something. Thank God you did."

"You are a foolish, foolish girl," he softly scolded, "and I do mean girl. That's certainly not the behavior of a smart, capable woman who runs her own cafe."

"I know. I'm really embarrassed."

"What were you thinking?"

"I guess I wasn't. I was too worried about you."

"We'll talk about this later. Did you twist your ankle tryin' to get down the hill?"

"Uh-huh. I was exhausted and I lost my balance."

"I'm gonna pull off your boot. Are you ready?"

"Okay, go ahead."

As carefully as he could, Luke began, and though she gasped and winced, the footwear finally came off. Peeling back her sock, he studied the swollen joint.

"It's not too bad. You need to ice it for twenty minutes, then soak in a hot bath. I'll wrap it when you're done. You should be feeling better by tomorrow."

"A hot bath," she repeated with a moan. "That sounds heavenly. I feel so grubby, and I'm achy and cold. I swear I've wrenched every muscle in my body."

"I'll fill the tub for you," he declared, standing up. "Hopefully there'll be some Epsom salts in the bathroom."

TESS WATCHED HIM MARCH away, then closed her eyes, thinking what a narrow escape she'd had. Hitting her head had been frightening, but when she'd stood up and he'd disappeared, she'd been truly terrified. Though she'd tried to run, her boots weren't made for either the terrain or for jogging, and she'd tripped more than once. When she'd finally caught sight of him in the distance, she'd literally cried with re-lief.

"Your bath is runnin.'"

His voice snatched her attention, and looking up she gave him a grateful smile.

"Thank you, Luke, so much, and you were right. I feel like I'm ten years old and just did something very bad."

"I'm sure you do, and you did. Wait one-second. I'll get you something to drink."

"Where would I go, and how would I get there?"

Pausing his step, he turned and looked back at her.

"Sounds like you're already feelin' better."

"I'm definitely better than when I was lying in the snow on the side of that hill."

"Good to hear," he said with a grin, then shooting her a wink, he walked away.

"Hurry back," she called after him.

But her unexpected surge of energy was short-lived. A wave of fa-tigue swept through her body, and closing her eyes, she was drifting into sleep when he returned. In one hand he carried a glass of water, and in the other a bag of frozen peas. Accepting the drink, she popped the as-pirin into her mouth, then discovering how thirsty she was, she gulped down the entire glass.

"Thank you. Wow. I didn't know how badly I need that."

"You're welcome," he replied, sitting at her feet and molding the packet of vegetables around her ankle. "I'll do this until the tub's ready," then pausing, he asked, "Tess, where's your car?"

"I hadn't thought about that," she said sheepishly. "It's where you saw it, at the entrance to the woods."

"That's what I thought," he muttered. "We might still have time to cover your tracks."

"Sorry."

"Say that one more time and your butt will hurt worse than your head and your ankle."

"But I am."

"I know, that's why you don't have to keep sayin' it," he retorted, pulling his phone from his pocket.

"Who are you calling?"

"Robbie. I just hope the call goes through and he picks up."

"Did you make it?" Robbie asked, answering on the first ring. "Are you settled in at the lodge?"

"Hey, Robbie. Yep, I made it, but Tess followed me out here. She left her car on the dirt road at the thicket near the train station. Do you know where I mean?"

"Sure. I used to go hiking through those woods."

"There's no way she can get back there. She's sprained her ankle."

"Oh, no!"

"Oh, yes! She can call her assistant manager to cover for her at the cafe, but we've got to get that car back to her place."

"Does she have the keys with her?"

"Shit, the keys," Luke grunted.

"I have a hide-a-key under the left back wheel well," Tess piped up, "and there's a key to the house by the back door under a green flower pot."

"Thank God. What about the remote for the garage?"

"It's the second button on the rearview mirror."

Luke quickly repeated the information to Robbie.

"Leave this to me," Robbie said confidently. "I'll handle it, no problem."

"Hang on a second," Luke said, walking across the room to stare out the window. "It's gettin' dark. I think you should drive to the lumber yard and park. There's a back door that's always left open. Do you know the one?"

"Yep, I sure do."

"Go in the yard, then sneak out through that back door. You can jog from there to Tess's car. It can't be more than a mile. When you reach Tess's house, run inside and turn on the bedroom and living room lights."

"But what about turnin' them off?"

"You're gonna have to go back later. Sorry, but I don't know any other way. It has to seem like she's there."

"Don't worry, I'll take care of it."

"One more thing. Jeb will know I'm not on that train to Longville by now, and he would've alerted his deputies. They'll be out on patrol."

"Okay. I'll keep my eyes open."

"Thanks again, Robbie."

"No problem. I'm glad I can finally do something to help. I'll let you know when I'm done."

"Great. Bye."

"Bye, Luke."

Ending the call, Luke walked back to Tess and stared down at her, a heavy frown crossing his brow.

"You're in a whole heap of trouble, young lady."

"I know," she murmured, "but can you save the lecture until later?"

"Uh-huh, but you can be thinkin' about it in the meantime. That tub's probably ready."

"Thank goodness. I can't seem to get warm. I thought I was going to freeze to death when you found me."

Lifting the packet of peas from her ankle, he picked her up, carried her to the bathroom, and placed her carefully on the edge of the tub.

"Do you need help gettin' those clothes off?" he asked, turning off the faucets.

"Just my jeans."

"Stand up on your one good foot and I'll help you over to the wall. You can lean back and I'll slide them off you."

But moments later, as he shimmied her jeans and panties down her legs, his cock stirred at the sight of her perfectly trimmed, beautifully curly bush. Doing his best to ignore his reaction, he lifted her sweater over her head, then her T-shirt, only to discover she wasn't wearing a bra.

"I find them uncomfortable," she confessed, a smile crossing her face.

"Hey, that works for me," he said with a chuckle, staring down at her luscious breasts as he willed his manhood to settle down. "You need to get in the tub before I jump on your bones. I'll help you over there, then sit on the edge and slide in, but hold on to me while you're doin' it."

With his help, she managed to sink into the hot, inviting water, and lying back, she let out a long, grateful breath.

"You rest there a while," he said, enjoying the sight of her naked body. "I'll be back to get you in a bit. If you need me just yell. I need to check what supplies are here, and I wanna make sure Ghost is okay, but don't you dare try to get out of that bath by yourself, you hear me?"

"Yes, Luke, I hear you, and I won't."

Moving back to the living room, he picked up the melting peas, and after returning them to the freezer, he found one of three beers left in the fridge. Gratefully dropping down at the kitchen table and taking a long drink, he shook his head. Tess had followed him all the way to the lodge on foot. Though he was upset, it had been an act of courage and fortitude...and love.

"I promise, I'll prove my innocence," he murmured. "I just hope I'll live through it. Tyler Anderson is one dangerous man."

CHAPTER EIGHT

SITTING IN THE LOCAL tavern nursing a beer, Dwayne gazed across at the many bottles lined up behind the bar. He wasn't looking at them, but staring forward, lost in his thoughts. Kevin, the bartender, had watched Dwayne grow up, and in spite of being dealt a tough hand of cards, Dwayne was easy going, generally happy, and took things in stride. It was clear whatever was troubling the young deputy had to be serious. Moving closer and standing in front of him, Kevin hoped Dwayne would start talking. When he remained quiet, Kevin decided to push.

"Hey, Dwayne, do you wanna talk about it?"

"Huh?" Dwayne muttered, darting his eyes to Kevin.

"Whatever's on your mind, do you wanna talk about it?"

Dwayne looked around, and though there was no-one in earshot, he leaned across the bar and lowered his voice.

"What's a fella to do?" he began slowly, sporting a pained expression. "I mean, if a fella knows something, and he should tell, but if he does it'll get another person in real bad trouble when they shouldn't be, what's a fella to do?"

"Let me get this straight," Kevin said patiently. "You have information about someone, and if you share it, that someone will be in trouble, but they're not guilty of anything. Is that what you're sayin'?"

"Yep, that's about the gist of it."

"Do what you think is right. If that means keeping what you know to yourself, then that's what you should do."

"It's all so wrong," Dwayne mumbled, shaking his head.

"What is?" Kevin asked. "Now you're confusin' me."

"What happened to this other fella," Dwayne replied with a heavy frown. "It's all so wrong."

"If that's the case, you should try to make it right."

Dwayne stared at him, his brow deeply furrowed as he thought about the advice, then suddenly broke into a broad grin.

"That's it!" Dwayne exclaimed excitedly. "That's what I'm gonna do, dang it. Thanks, buddy."

"I'm glad I could help."

"You did, Kevin. Lordy, you did," Dwayne declared, then clambering off his bar stool, he strode purposefully out the door.

Driving from the tavern, trying to think of a way to help Luke Larson clear his name, he spotted Robbie's bright red truck pulling into the local lumber yard. Impulsively hitting his brakes, Dwayne swung into an awkward turn, missed the driveway, bounced over the curb and into the parking lot, but miraculously reached the truck just as Robbie climbed out.

"Hey," Dwayne yelled, waving his arm.

"Uh, hello," Robbie replied warily. "Do I know you?"

"Not officially, I mean, we've seen each other around and such. I'm Dwayne Johnson, the Sheriff's nephew."

DWAYNE WAS HURRYING towards him. Though he tired to remain calm, Robbie's stomach churned as he leaned back against his truck.

"Is there something I can help you with?" he asked as Dwayne approached.

The young deputy stared at him for a minute, glanced around the busy parking lot, then jerked his head towards his car.

"Uh, could you sit with me for a minute?"

"Sorry, Dwayne, but I'm really pressed for time. There's somethin' I've gotta do, and I've gotta do it right now."

"If it has anythin' to do with Luke Larson I wanna help," Dwayne declared in a loud whisper.

"What? Why would you say that?" Robbie stammered, his face growing hot.

"I really think you should get in my car. There are too many people around. They might hear us."

Though his heart had started thumping, and he was completely bewildered, Robbie realized he had no choice. Reluctantly stepping around Dwayne's car, he climbed into the passenger's seat, while Dwayne settled behind the wheel.

"Okay," Robbie said, hoping he didn't sound as anxious as he felt, "why don't you tell me what's on your mind."

"Sure, okay. The thing is, I may be a deputy, but I'm on your side."

Robbie paused.

"I'm not sure I understand," he murmured cautiously.

"Sure, sorry, this has been confusin' for me too, and I don't always talk well. I know the guys at the station laugh about me, and my uncle, he says bein' a deputy will make me a man, but I don't wanna be a deputy, I wanna work with animals. I like animals, and animals like me back. They trust me, and I understand them. Do you know what I mean?"

"I do, Dwayne," Robbie replied, still confounded by the odd conversation. "I feel that way about animals too, and I'm sorry you're havin' a hard time bein' a cop, but I really need to know what you want from me."

"Like I said, I wanna help you and Luke. I was at his ranch earlier, and I heard you guys talkin' inside the barn. I know Luke's at the Anderson's huntin' lodge, and he didn't do what everyone claims. I wanna help you both so he can be a free man again. I wanna catch whoever set him up, I really do. It's only right."

Though the young man seemed completely sincere, Robbie eyed him skeptically.

"You don't believe me," Dwayne muttered, a deep frown crossing his brow. "Is that because I'm the sheriff's nephew?"

"This is just...unexpected...and, Dwayne, you're a cop."

"But like I said, I heard you talkin'. Luke didn't hit old Nate on the head and steal that money," he declared earnestly. "When I heard that, I thought, Luke Larson is an innocent man. I didn't know what to do, so I went and had a drink and talked to Kevin at the tavern. He made me realize I had to make things right."

"You didn't tell Kevin what you overheard, or where Luke is, did you?" Robbie asked anxiously, his heart leaping.

"What? Of course not," Dwayne exclaimed, his eyebrows lifting.

"Sorry," Robbie said quickly, "it just scared me when you said that."

"It's okay. I know I can be a bit slow sometimes, but I'm not that bad."

"No, of course not. My apologies."

"So, uh, will you let me help you? Please? It's so bad what happened."

"Yes, Dwayne, you can definitely help," Robbie replied, relief flooding his body, "and I'm very grateful. In fact, there's something you can do for Luke and me right now. Is there any chance you can take me to the entrance of the woods near the train station?"

SOAKING IN THE HOT bath until the water had turned tepid, Tess finally felt the chill leave her body. Helping her out, Luke dried her off as she rested her hands on his shoulders.

"Damn, girl, you are so beautiful," he murmured huskily, then pressed his lips on her in a soft, long, lingering kiss.

"Take me to bed," she moaned as he pulled back. "I want you so much."

"Darlin', you've had a rough time of it, and I need to take care of that ankle."

"My ankle will be fine."

"Yeah, because I'll see to it!"

Sweeping her up and carrying her to the bedroom, he sat her on the edge of the bed.

"There used to be thick, fleece robes in these closets for guests," he said, walking across the room and opening a door. "Yep, just like always."

Sliding it off the hanger, he hurried it back to her and draped it around her shoulders.

"Slip your arms into that. I'll be right back."

"Where are you going?"

"I'm just gonna fetch the medicine bag. Slide back and prop yourself up on some pillows. Do you want anything else while I'm out there? How about some brandy?"

"Yes, please, Brandy would be wonderful. Will you join me?"

"You bet."

Watching his tall, broad frame stride from the room, Tess was filled with relief and gratitude. Like a gallant white knight he'd come to her rescue, and once again she cursed herself for doubting him.

Anger bubbled up.

"It was all your doing, Jeb," she muttered furiously as she slipped into the bathrobe and shimmied herself up the bed. "You turned me against him. You decided he was guilty from day one. Why? Why did you do that, and why did I listen to you?"

"First sign of insanity. That's what they say when you start talkin' to yourself," Luke declared, walking in carrying two brandy snifters in one hand, and the medicine bag in the other. "You sure sound mad."

"I am mad. I'm not going insane, but I am mad."

"You wanna tell me about it?" he asked, placing the glasses on the nightstand. "Take a sip, that'll calm you down."

"I'm mad at Jeb, and I'm mad at myself," she admitted, sipping on the brandy as he sat on the bed next to her foot.

"Why are you mad at Jeb?"

"Why do you think? He decided to be judge and jury. He had no right."

"I reckon there's more to it than that," Luke remarked, pouring a pungent liquid on a gauze pad and wiping it over her ankle.

"What is that stuff?"

"Horse liniment, but it works great on humans too," he replied, smiling up at her. "Answer the question."

"You didn't ask me anything."

"Don't be a smart-ass."

"Okay," she said with a resigned sigh. "I'm mad at him for a lot of reasons, but mostly convincing me you were guilty."

"Uh-huh," Luke grunted, picking up an ace bandage from the medicine box. "You wanna explain how he did that?"

"He was relentless. He kept going on and on about the evidence. He didn't quit. It's all I heard."

"I think you're more mad at yourself than him."

Not sure what to say she didn't respond, and sat silently watching him bandage her ankle.

"There you go, Tess. It's not a bad sprain. You'll heal fast."

"You're right," she murmured. "I shouldn't have been so weak. I'm sorry, Luke. Truly."

"I know you are, darlin.'"

"Do you forgive me?"

"There's nothin' to forgive. It was a rough time for everyone, and you were upset about the business with Patty. That didn't help, but it's in the past, and we have to look ahead. Speakin' of mistakes," he said, placing the bag on the floor and moving to sit next to her, "you were supposed to go home."

"Uh, yeah."

"But now you're here, and there are loose ends to tie up. You need to call the cafe and tell your assistant manager you've come down with a horrible cold and you won't be in for a few days."

"The cafe! Shit! What's wrong with me?"

"Maybe your brain froze on that long hike."

"It must have," she muttered, shaking her head. "I'm such an idiot sometimes."

"We're all capable of being idiots," he said with a grin.

"But that was so stupid. She'll be wondering where I am."

"I'm sure she will. Call her right now, then get in touch with your brother and tell him the same thing. Make sure he knows not to bring you chicken soup."

"Okay, but that might be difficult."

"You'd better make sure he doesn't. Where's your phone?"

"In my jeans pocket."

"Before I fetch it—Tess—for the record—I'm very upset with you."

"I know, and I don't blame you."

"Having said that," he continued, lowering his voice, "you followed me all the way out here, and you weren't even dressed for the weather."

"Well, yeah, I was worried sick."

"Honestly, darlin', I don't know what to say. You're somethin' special, and I'll never forget this, not ever."

"Luke..."

"But you'd better not do anything that crazy ever again."

"I won't, or at least, I'll try not to."

"I'm gonna fetch your phone."

Softly kissing her, he felt the sudden urge to peel the clothes off her fragrant body and utterly devour her, but managing to resist the temptation, he straightened up and left the room.

CHAPTER NINE

ENTERING THE BATHROOM and picking up Tess's jeans, Luke's expression grew grim. Finding the evidence he needed to clear his name wouldn't be easy, and if he was caught, he'd end up in prison with an even longer sentence.

"How the hell am I gonna do this?" he muttered. "Lord, if you're of a mind to send out miracles, I sure could use one."

Taking her clothes into the guest room, he found her phone in the jeans pocket, and carried it back to the lounge. While she made the call, he checked the basement wine cellar and found it still boasted a generous collection. Finding a bottle of Cabernet, he poured them both a glass in the kitchen and returned with them to the living room. She'd finished the call, but as he handed her the crystal goblet, his phone rang.

"My turn," he declared, lifting it from his shirt pocket. "Hello Robbie."

"How is everything, Luke?"

"Interesting," he replied. "I have a house guest."

"Excuse me? Did you say house guest? Wait, are you talkin' about that big feral cat that used to hang around the barn? I'm surprised he's still alive."

"I'll keep my eye out for him, but no. Tess followed me here," Luke replied, shooting her a frown. "She banged her head and twisted her ankle on the journey. I found her lying in the snow on top of that slope above the lodge."

"Thank goodness you spotted her," Robbie exclaimed. "She could've frozen to death."

"Yep, she could've, but luckily I did, and now she's on the mend, sittin' here like a princess sippin' wine with her feet up. What about you? What's happening there?"

"I have some amazing news. You won't believe this. Do you remember Dwayne, the sheriff's nephew?"

"Of course. A bit slow, but a good kid."

"He overheard us talkin', and he wants to help you clear your name."

Luke paused.

"Luke? Did you hear me?"

"Oh, yeah, I heard you, but it sounds like a set up."

"It's not. He went to great lengths to tell me how difficult it had been to figure out what he should do, and I believe him. He gave it a great deal of thought and came up with an idea, though Tess is with you now, so it probably won't matter. He's standing right here. Talk to him yourself."

"Robbie, I'm not sure if—"

"Hello, Luke. Dwayne here."

"Hi, Dwayne. I understand you want to help me clear my name."

"Yes, Luke I do, I really do."

"I'm sure you'll understand if I'm skeptical."

"Huh?"

"You're law enforcement Dwayne."

"Yeah, I'm a deputy."

"So, uh, it's difficult for me to trust you."

"Oh, I get it," Dwayne muttered. "Yeah, but see—upholdin' the law is doin' what's right, and you got sent away and that wasn't right, so doin' what's right is findin' the guy who hurt poor old Nate, and you can't do that locked up, so I want to help you put things right."

Luke chuckled.

"That sounds great, Dwayne, thank you. Robbie said you have an idea."

"I sure do," Dwayne said, his voice full of enthusiasm. "I have a dog called Rex. If you want to stay with Tess, I can tell Jeb I'd like to hang out at her place and be her bodyguard instead of watching her house parked on the street. Rex is real big with a scary bark, but he's super sweet. Jeb will think she's being protected, and you can stay there without worrying about him coming over all the time to check on her."

"Robbie, that's an excellent suggestion," Luke said thoughtfully, "but Tess is with me now, and she's twisted her ankle. She can't get home even if she wanted to. She's already called the cafe and told them she's sick, and she'll be telling Jeb the same thing, but we're worried he'll go by her house and try to see her. Dwayne, if you could offer to stay with her, and pretend she's there, that would be terrific. Do you think you can do that?"

"Sure. I'd love to do that. If anyone comes over with soup or something, I can answer the door and say she's too sick to get out of bed. I know Jeb will go for it. It will be one less thing for him to think about. He's always complaining he's got too much on his plate."

"Dwayne, you're a Godsend. Thank you! You truly are saving the day."

"I am?"

"Yes, you are. If anything should happen and you need to reach me, call Robbie," Luke said, not wanting his number on Dwayne's phone. "I may be reachable, but Robbie will be available and can help if there's any trouble."

"Okay. I'm so glad I can help you. I never did believe you were guilty."

"Thank you, Dwayne. I appreciate that."

"Tell Tess I said hi."

"I sure will, and thanks again. Would you put Robbie back on, please."

"Sure, here you go."

"Hey, Luke. See, I told you."

"Yeah, you did. Funny thing, I was just prayin' for a miracle, and it's happened. I'll speak to you in the morning, assumin' nothing happens overnight. Just make sure Dwayne heads over to Tess's house right away."

"Will do. Stay safe."

"Thanks, Robbie, you too."

As Luke ended the call, Tess stared up at him with a wide smile.

"You're right. That truly is a miracle," she declared. "Dwayne is a bit slow, but he's got a big heart and he keeps his word. He won't let you down."

"I know. He kept saying he had to help me because it was the right thing to do. If everyone thought like he did, the world would be a better place."

"Amen to that," she said with a sigh.

"I'm gonna rustle us up dinner. Don't go anywhere."

"Are you kidding? I wouldn't dare, even if I wanted to."

LUKE COOKED THEM UP spaghetti, but exhausted from her arduous afternoon, by the end of the meal Tess was yawning. Quickly cleaning up the dishes, he helped her hobble to the guest room, and as she slipped out of the bathrobe and into bed, he quickly stripped and climbed in next to her.

"Sure feels like the tide is turnin'," he remarked.

"I hope so," she murmured, snuggling against him. "It feels so good to have you next to me."

"How's your head," he asked, moving his fingers across her forehead.

"It hurts a bit."

"And your ankle?"

"That hurts too, but I know what will take my mind off the pain," she said softly, wrapping her fingers around his cock.

Closing his eyes, he let out a low groan.

"You really do need a spankin' and a whole lotta lovin'."

"I do," she moaned, sliding her hand up and down his stiffening shaft. "I need all of it."

"Roll over, but be careful. Watch that ankle."

Helping her move so her back was to him, he clutched her breasts as he rested his cock against her full, plump backside.

"You've got such a gorgeous ass," he crooned, "and you know it's gonna be real red, real soon."

His whispered threat sent a surge of wet heat through her pussy, and as he tweaked her nipples, she thrust back against him.

"Not too red I hope," she whimpered. "I'm injured."

He chuckled.

"Nope. Like I said, real red, real soon," he repeated, pinching her cherry tips again.

She gasped, then placed her fingers against her sex.

"Please, Luke, please, please slide inside me?"

"Since you said please three times, but you'd better move your hand from that pussy, or I'll have to say no."

"Oh, sorry, sorry," she whispered hastily, jerking her arm back.

Slowly impaling her, he drove deep inside her wet channel with a single, powerful stroke, evoking a long, whimpering moan. Staying buried for several long seconds, he pressed a finger against her clit, rubbing vigorously, then began thrusting with strong, urgent strokes. Spurred on by her utterances of pleasure, he quickened his pace, pinching her nipples offering unpredictable bursts of exquisite pain. Each time he sensed her nearing her climax, he'd pause to nuzzle her neck, and whisper wicked promises of shackles, crops, and vibrators.

"Please, don't make me wait any more," she finally begged. "I can't stand it. I need to come."

"Will you be a good girl?" he whispered, squeezing her breasts. "No more impetuous risk-takin'?"

"I will, I promise. I won't do anything crazy again, I swear."

Holding her tightly, he let loose, pumping aggressively, his finger continuing to torment her clit.

"Luke, I'm there," she gasped. "I'm going to...."

Letting out a wild wail, waves of shuddering spasms suddenly possessed her, rippling through her sex and shooting sparks through her body. Her orgasm hurtled him into his. Clamping her hips against him, convulsions shuddered through his loins, and as he groaned through his euphoria, his member jerked inside her, ejecting his hot essence.

"Is this all some amazing dream?" she murmured as he slipped from her depths. "Am I going to wake up?"

"I sure as hell hope not," he muttered, "cos if you do, I will too, and that will really piss me off."

"I don't think I've ever been happier than at this moment, or more scared," she murmured softly, rolling over to face him. "I couldn't bear it if anything happened to you. What if they find you before you can get the proof you need to expose the person who set you up?"

"Everything will work itself out," he said quietly, "but Tess, over the next few days I'm gonna have to take some risks, and I can't be worried about you. You've gotta promise you won't do anything reckless, and I mean it. You've gotta stay here. If someone comes knockin', ignore it unless you're sure it's Dwayne or Robbie."

"I understand, I do. I'm really sorry about what I did...though...lying here with you like this, if I'm being honest, I have no regrets."

"Yeah, well, you got lucky. Things might have ended badly."

"I realize that," she admitted, lowering her eyes. "If I'd known you were traveling so far I probably would have gone home, but what do you want me to do if someone shows up here?"

"In the mornin' we'll scout out a good hidin' place. If you get an unwelcome visitor, that's where you'll go, and when it's safe you'll call me."

"Okay. Uh, Luke?"

"Yeah, darlin'?"

"Am I'm forgiven?"

"Sure, you're forgiven, but I told you to get your ass home and you promised me you would. You broke that promise and came after me. There's nothin' you can say that'll get you outta the trouble you're in. You deserve to be punished, and you know it."

"You're right," she whispered, a red blush crossing her face.

"That's something at least."

"What?"

"You didn't start with the excuses again," he said with a sigh. "Now it's time for both of us to get some rest."

"Yes, I'm totally wipe out, but Luke?"

"Hmmm?"

"I may be in a heap of trouble, but I'm still really glad I'm here."

"You may not say that in a couple of days when you're over my knee," he muttered, "now go to sleep."

"I don't care," she whispered. "I wouldn't trade this moment for anything."

CHAPTER TEN

IT HAD TAKEN LUKE ONLY fifteen minutes to ride over the gentle hills and across the paddocks separating the Anderson family compound from the hunting lodge. With plenty of trees for cover he had no concerns about being spotted, and staring across the last empty field, he studied the home of his nemesis, Tyler Anderson.

He assumed Tyler would be at his father's office. The family owned several businesses, and the small empire was run from a modest building in the center of town. Tyler was second-in-command to his dad, but Luke had never thought Tyler's ability matched that of his entrepreneurial father.

Keeping a sharp watch for anyone approaching, or any movement inside the house, he moved closer, but a growing doubt began to take hold. He didn't believe Tyler had the guts or the brainpower to pull off such an elaborate scheme, but he had chased Tess for years. Everyone knew he'd been furious Tess had passed him over for a small time rancher.

"Maybe I've always underestimated you," Luke muttered as he approached. "Someone set me up, and if it wasn't you, who was it?"

Finally reaching the back door of the house, Luke slid from the saddle and wrapped the reins loosely around the hitching post, though it wasn't necessary. Ghost wouldn't go anywhere, and if he did take a wander in search of grass beneath the snow, a whistle would bring him running back.

"I won't be long," he purred stroking the horse's neck. "You keep a look out."

Grinning at the thought of Ghost whinnying if someone approached, Luke moved to the back door and tried the handle. It turned in his hand, but he wasn't surprised. Tyler had no reason to lock his house. The compound was secure, and Tyler wouldn't imagine anyone riding in from the back fields. Stepping quietly inside, Luke paused to listen. The only sound was the loud ticking of a clock.

"Man, that'd drive me crazy," he murmured, moving through the gleaming, stainless steel kitchen.

The house was sprawling, impressively furnished with large rooms. Hastening his step, he searched out an office, hoping to find a diary or appointment book. Finally discovering a study off a wide hallway, he walked quickly behind the desk and let out a grunt of triumph. Sitting in front of him was a day planner. Taking the thin piece of red ribbon hanging from the bottom, he flipped open the leather-bound book. Tyler's appointments for the day were written in red ink.

"Thank the Lord," he muttered. "Someone else who doesn't use a smartphone. I thought I was the only person left who kept a regular diary like this."

Reading through the notes it showed Tyler in meetings until early afternoon. Though still nervous about snooping around the house, the information gave Luke a semblance of reassurance. Turning back the pages, he searched out the date his world had been turned upside down.

The day he'd met Patty Jamison.

The day poor old Nate had been attacked and robbed.

His pulse ticked up.

The unforgettable date stared up at him.

Heart racing, he began to read.

His heart sank.

Dinner - 6:30 - Red Lion - poker - back room. Doug, Will, Jeb, Johnny and Bob. $10k Min.

"Dammit! He was at a poker game," Luke grunted, "although...this doesn't mean he was actually there. Maybe he hired someone to clobber Nate and plant that stuff in my garage."

Dropping into the desk chair, he let out a heavy sigh and shook his head. He didn't believe Tyler would be cold-blooded enough to pay someone to attack the old man. It could happen in a moment of panic, but not a pre-meditated assault.

"But if it wasn't you, Tyler, who the hell was it?"

Staring around the room he saw photographs of loved ones, past girlfriends, and the celebrity visitors who had been guests at the ranch.

Slowly rising to his feet, he ambled across the room to study the smiling faces, and in the background of one of the photographs he spotted Patty Jamison.

"Dare I risk talking to you?" he mumbled, staring at the attractive girl. "You lied back then, but do I have a choice? I have to get the information from you. There's no-one else."

Striding from the den and back through the house, he walked outside and up to his horse waiting patiently at the old-fashioned hitching post.

"Where do I go from here, Ghost?"

The horse's big brown eyes stared back at him.

"If only you could speak English," Luke said softly, then swung himself into the saddle.

Riding back to the hunting lodge, he tried to think who else might have had an axe to grind. Except for Patty, who seemed incapable of doing something so nasty to old Nate, there was only Tyler. By the time he reached the lodge, he knew he had to verify Tyler's presence at the poker game.

The morning was clear and sunny. Luke decided to risk putting Ghost in a small paddock behind the barn. With his white coat, the horse blended in with the thin layer of snow still covering the ground.

Pulling off the saddle and bridle, the happy horse began bucking and playing, happy to be free.

"I'm so glad you're back!"

Turning around, he spotted Tess waving from the back door wearing a large, black wool shirt. He broke into a smile and strode quickly forward, lifting her off her feet and swinging her around.

"You look so much better," he declared. "Where did you get that shirt?"

"I dug it out of a closet in one of the bedrooms. My clothes still haven't dried."

"I'm not surprised," he remarked, setting her down gently. "How's your ankle?"

"Hardly bothering me at all. The cut on my head hurts more, but I don't have a headache. Considering what I went through, I feel fine."

"I knew you'd bounce back," he said with a grin. "That breakfast you ate this mornin' told me you were feelin' better, even if you were bleary-eyed."

"I was starving," she exclaimed as they walked inside. "I can't believe there's so much food in this place. I thought no-one came out here during winter."

"I'm startin' to worry about that. Used to be no-one did, but findin' that milk and eggs in the refrigerator in the garage was a bit of a shock."

"Do you think it's safe to stay here?" she asked, her voice tinged with concern. "Maybe someone is using it and they'll come back."

"I'm thinkin' along the same lines. Last night we had no choice, but now I'm wonderin' if we should make a move," he remarked as they settled on the couch. "Maybe the Anderson's have hired a caretaker. It always took some cleanin' when we opened back up in the spring."

"We could always go back to my place," she suggested. "With Dwayne there, no-one would think for a minute you'd be staying with me."

"You might be right," he said thoughtfully. "I've done what I came out here to do, and you can't pretend to be sick forever."

"What happened at Tyler's? Were you able to get inside?"

"It was almost too easy."

"It was? That's great. What did you find out?"

"Unfortunately, according to Tyler's diary, he had a poker game scheduled at the Red Lion, that doesn't mean he was there."

"Oh, my, gosh!" she suddenly exclaimed, "I'm such an idiot."

"Yep, you proved that yesterday, but what are you talkin' about?"

"I'm so sorry, Luke. I just remembered! Jeb won a bunch of money off him that night. He was giving me the details when he got the call about Nate."

"Damn, girl, it sure would have been helpful if you'd mentioned that sooner."

"When Jeb told me at the time, I didn't give it a second thought. I only remembered now because you mentioned a poker game. Shoot, I'm really sorry."

"Hey, it's okay, and I'm sorry I snapped," he apologized. "Better late than never, and now I know he was there. I guess I'm just frustrated. If he was at that poker game, it means someone else is behind this, but who could it be? I sure as hell don't know anyone who hates me that much. Quite honestly, I didn't think Tyler did, but he was the only person I could think of who was mad at me at the time."

"Seems to me there's only one person who can tell you what you need to know. The person who got you up to the lake, and then lied about what you did while you were there."

"Patty Jamison," Luke muttered, a deep frown crossing his face.

"Yep, Patty Jamison."

"How the hell am I gonna get Patty to tell me who persuaded her to call me out that night?" he said with a heavy sigh.

"I don't know, but you'll think of something. Would you like some coffee?"

"Maybe in a minute."

"Not meaning to change the subject, but I really like this shirt," she said, running her hand over the thick, black wool. "I'm almost tempted to take it with me."

"Oh, sure, that's a great idea," he said sarcastically. "Steal a shirt from our hide-out."

"I was only kidding," she declared, then pausing, she murmured, "Luke, aren't you glad I'm here? You wouldn't know that Tyler was at the poker game if I hadn't followed you."

"And I wouldn't be sittin' here worried about gettin' outta this place before someone finds us and you get your cute butt thrown behind bars."

"Oh, well, yeah, I guess that's true too—but isn't it worth it?"

"I don't have an answer for that yet. When this is all over, if you're still runnin' your cafe, then yeah. But if you're sittin' in a jail cell, the answer will be a resoundin' no. Does that—"

But the sound of his phone snatched his attention before he could finish.

"Hey, Robbie, what's the latest?" he asked urgently. "Is everything okay?"

"It's good news," Robbie replied. "Dwayne just called. Jeb thinks you jumped from the train somewhere between here and Longville."

"Seriously? It would've been an option if I'd wanted to break my leg, but I guess that didn't occur to them."

"Apparently they had a big talk about that. They decided you must have bailed when the train slowed going through one of the stations. There's a major search underway."

Luke chuckled.

"I wish them luck, and now I have some news for you. Someone has been at this lodge recently and I'm worried they might be back. Tess and I are gonna head outta here. We'll be at my barn tonight. Can you let Dwayne know?"

"Yeah, sure, but don't wait too long."

"It's a tough call. I'm not sure I wanna ride up to my property in broad daylight, but stayin' until later is a risk too."

"I see what you mean," Robbie murmured. "Whatever you decide, just call me when you're on your way and I'll make sure I'm there."

"Will do. Thanks, Robbie."

"Stay safe, Luke. See you soon."

Ending the call and placing the phone on the coffee table, Luke turned and picked up Tess's hands.

"Young lady," he said firmly, "we'll be leavin', but before we go, you and I have some unfinished business."

A hot, red blush flared across her cheeks.

"But, uh, shouldn't we, uh, get out of here now?"

"Like I just said to Robbie, it's a risk either way, but movin' back to my place in the dark is the safest bet. It's the middle of the week. If someone is usin' this lodge it's probably durin' the weekend. I'm gonna take care of you right now."

CHAPTER ELEVEN

TESS PROTESTED, FLIRTED, then begged, but Luke was unmoved, and when he clutched her hair and asked if she deserved a spanking, with a deep sigh she'd nodded her head.

Ordering her to take off the black wool shirt, he removed his belt, tied her wrists, and instructed her to lie over his lap. As she awkwardly crawled into position, he placed his heavy leg over the backs of hers, and held her firmly at the waist.

"Tess, do I need to scold you again?"

"Uh, yes," she bleated. "I think you should."

"I expected that," he replied. "Another attempt to put off the inevitable. If you need to be reminded about why you're over my knee I'm happy to oblige, but I'll do it while I'm whippin' your ass."

"Luke, wait," she shouted with a wriggle. "Can't we talk about this?"

"Nope, no more waitin', and if you try to put me off one more time you'll get ten extra swats at the end. Understand?"

"Yes, I understand, but I only followed you because I was worried. If something had happened to you on the journey—"

"Enough!" he said sternly. "And it's Yes, *Sir*."

"Sorry. Yes, Sir."

His large, rough hand had been resting on her right cheek, and raising it in the air, he sent it down with a hard swat.

"Ow!"

"You broke your promise and you put yourself at grave risk. That's not allowed," he declared, landing several hard smacks in quick succession.

. "Ow, ouch ow."

"Shush, you were a very bad girl," he scolded, continuing to rain his slaps as she yelped. "You're going to learn what happens to very bad girls."

"Ow, I swear I won't—"

But a flurry of stinging swats from his flattened palm sent her into cries of pain. Though she tried to kick, her legs were no match for the strength of his, and when she tried to wriggle her hands from the belt it proved impossible. His hard, calloused hand persisted, flying from cheek to cheek, turning her skin bright pink.

"Ooh, Sir," she wailed, "it burns. You're spanking me so hard! Please, I can't take anymore."

Reminding himself it was the first proper spanking she'd ever had, he paused his hand and began rubbing her scalded backside.

"Will you do as you're told from now on? I'm not foolin' around Tess. These are dangerous days, and I'm not gonna let you end up in the slammer. Have you learned your lesson?"

"Yes, yes, I have, I swear," she gasped. "Really, I have."

"Why do I think you're sayin' that just so I won't spank you anymore?"

"I am! But I have learned, I promise," she swore urgently, "I'll do what you tell me from now on."

"Do I need to smack this red butt anymore?"

"No, no, you don't."

"If you'd said somethin' like, *that's up to you, Sir,* I might be inclined to believe you," he murmured thoughtfully, continuing to roam his hand over her scarlet skin. "Let's try that again. Do you think you've learned your lesson?"

"If you think so, Sir," she quickly replied.

"Do I need to spank this red butt anymore?"

"Ooh, Sir," she mewled, "that's up to you."

"See there, didn't it feel better when you put it like that? Did you feel the difference?"

"Yes, Sir, I did."

"I'd better make it stick. I'm gonna spank you some more so you understand that tryin' to convince me you've learned your lesson won't get you anywhere. I'll decide when you've had enough."

"Yes, Sir," she bleated, and though she was tempted to add, *please don't make it too hard,* she held her tongue.

Shifting her hips further across his lap, and tightening his grip around her waist, he sent his hand below her seat cheeks and whisked it upwards, catching the underside of her bottom with a series of stinging blows. She howled, but didn't ask him to stop. Repeating the action on the opposite side drew a hiss between her teeth. As he continued, the pale, tender skin quickly turned a blushing rose.

Clenching her teeth, Tess wondered when this second round would end. His relentless spanking kissed her skin with fire, his hold around her waist was like a vice, and she couldn't move her legs an inch. Dropping her head into the sofa cushion, she began to wail as his rough hand continued its punishing work. When he returned to the center of her cheeks, the sting on her sit spot remained a hot, burning prickle, more painful than his fresh slaps.

"So," he demanded loudly, "are we done? Have you learned your lesson?"

"If you think so, Sir," she panted. "I am very sorry for being so reckless."

"Do I need to spank you anymore?"

"That's up to you, Sir."

"Much better. I know your ass is real sore right now, but I want you to listen to me and listen good."

"Yes, Sir. I'm listening, Sir."

"If you disobey me about something so important again, I'm gonna smack your bottom even harder, and it will be a warm-up for my belt. Are we clear?"

"Ooh, Sir, yes, Sir, I don't want your belt."

"No, you don't, so you'd best behave. Stay like you are. I'm gonna rub you for a bit."

Smoothing his comforting caress across her burnt backside wouldn't alleviate the sting much, but it would help her relax and compose herself.

"Such a sorry girl."

"I am, I really am so sorry," she whimpered, but she couldn't help thinking her hot, stinging backside was worth the night she'd spent with him.

"You're gonna have to sit behind me on Ghost when we ride out tonight," he reminded her as he helped her curl up into this lap. "I don't think it's gonna be real comfortable for you."

"I walked all the way here, maybe I should walk back. I can't imagine sitting on anything."

"It's a few hours until we leave. You might feel differently by then."

"If someone had told me a month ago that I'd be on the run with a wanted cowboy, hiding out in the Anderson's ranch with my ass stinging like the blazes because he put me over his knee, I'd have told them they were ready for the looney bin."

"I gotta tell you, Tess, I still can't believe all this crap has happened," he remarked with a heavy sigh. "Except for gettin' in some trouble in my teens, which I guess happens to most kids, I've worked hard and done right by people. Just goes to show, you never know what life's gonna throw at you."

Curling against his chest she closed her eyes.

"It's not fair," she said softly. "The only reason I'm sittin' here with a sore ass is because someone framed you."

"No, Tess. The reason I spanked you good and hard is cos you broke a couple of important promises. You'd better fix your thinkin' girl."

"I suppose you're right."

"This is gonna end one way or another. I'll be able to get the truth outta Patty or I won't, and I've gotta feelin' I don't have long to do it."

"Luke, I feel really close to you right now. Will you please take me to the bedroom?"

"Sure, darlin'. A spankin' can do that, but there might be a time when I'll say no, or tease you a whole lot and still say no."

"Why?" she asked with a frown, lifting her head and staring at him with big eyes.

"Cos there's more than one way to punish a naughty girl. That's an old line, but it's as true today as the first time someone spoke it. Let's go," he said, shifting her off his lap, "but be careful. Remember your ankle."

Taking her hand and walking with her into the bedroom, he quickly stripped as she climbed on the bed.

"Get up on your hands and knees," he said huskily, admiring the tapestry of bright red blotches covering her backside.

"I'm so wet," she moaned, touching between her legs as he kneeled up behind her. "I don't remember ever feeling this needy."

A sweet, loving attitude had emerged, an almost little girl softness that he'd not seen before. A part of him wanted to draw out their lovemaking, and he would, but it would have to wait for another time. He sensed her urgency, and it was one he shared.

"Spread your legs, darlin', nice and wide."

As she shuffled her knees apart, he stared lustily at the glistening pussy between her thighs. Placing his cock in position and thrusting forward, he stroked slowly, relishing the feel of her delicious pussy wrapping around him, her succulent warm wetness, and her soft moans of pleasure.

"Feel good, darlin'?"

"Oh, Luke, so unbelievably good," she mewled. "Like...amazingly good."

Pumping with stronger thrusts as he gazed at her raspberry bottom, he could feel the shadow of his release, and he knew, if he kept up the pace, there would be no stopping the inevitable.

"Tell me when you're close," he panted as he slowed.

"Oh, Luke, please go back to what you were doing," she begged. "Fuck me hard."

She bucked back at him to underscore her lewd request, but rather than grant her wish, he buried himself in her depths and remained still, then pulling her cheek to the side, he touched her rosebud.

"Aaaah, Luke, no..."

Smiling, he released the cheek and withdrew his finger.

"Don't worry, Tess," he said softly. "You'll get there."

Mortified at the suggestion, she groaned in response, but grasping her waist he began pummeling her pussy. Her fingers curled around the sheets, and letting out a wild cry, she threw back her head. The pending release was big, and she wanted it desperately.

"I can feel you," he muttered, "you're chasin' your climax. Don't try, just let it wash over you."

Letting out a long breath she did as he said, focusing on his cock and his pelvis slapping against her hot, sore bottom. A tingling ripple moved through her body, slowly grew into a wave, then a tsunami, and she was abruptly at the crest.

Luke heard the catch of her breath and felt the sudden tightening of her womanhood. As her body grew taut and she let out a strange, high-pitched shriek, he dropped her hips and grabbed her plump cheeks, squeezing them as he fucked her with robust strokes.

His climax seized him.

It was a jerking, embracing release, the convulsions firing a wash of sensations through his body, until utterly spent, he slipped away. As she fell on her stomach, he collapsed next to her, out of breath and his heart pounding.

Closing his eyes, he felt her arm drop across his chest. He smiled as it landed, thinking how perfect they were together. Tess was everything he knew she would be, perhaps even more, and he yearned for the day his freedom would be returned and they could truly share a life together. But he still didn't know how that would happen. He didn't hold much hope that Patty would tell him the truth. There was no reason she should, and even if she did, there was no guarantee she'd repeat the information to the sheriff.

But as the post-orgasmic bliss began to engulf him, he had the vague inkling of an idea.

CHAPTER TWELVE

NIGHT WAS FALLING AND Luke had a problem. His saddle would leave no room for Tess to sit behind him. While the two of them could sit on Ghost bareback, Luke was loathe to leave his expensive saddle behind, and returning for it the following day was a risk he didn't want to take.

"I know exactly what to do," Tess proclaimed. "I'll go to my dad's and get Dusty."

"I assume Dusty is a horse," Luke said, "but where is she?"

"She's out in a pasture with some other horses. The ranch is next to this one, remember? She's only a couple of fields away, and no-one will even notice she's gone. All I need is a halter and lead rope. I ride her bareback all the time."

"You do? Tess Turner that's brilliant!"

She had washed her clothes, but they wouldn't offer enough protection for the cold night air. Luke relented and let her borrow the thick, wool shirt which cloaked her like a heavy winter coat.

"We still need to return it once this is all over, in person if need be."

"Of course," she agreed, then added wistfully, "but I do love it."

Not planning to go back inside the lodge, they made sure all trace of them had been erased, then climbed on Ghost and began the short ride to the back fields of the Turner ranch. In spite of her tender skin, sitting behind Luke with her arms around his waist and her head resting on his back, she was loving every minute of their trek. Watching the sky transform into a black slate with tiny pinpricks of light, she felt herself being lulled into a calm peace, and she could think of nowhere on earth she'd rather be.

Luke too, was delighting in the short journey. In spite of their earlier lovemaking, Tess's body pressing against him stirred his cock. If they'd had a blanket, he would have pulled her to the ground and ravaged her under the sparkling diamond sky and silver crescent moon.

"When this is over, I'm gonna take you and a couple of shag throws to the back paddocks at my ranch."

"A nighttime picnic?" she whispered, lifting her head and placing her lips to his ear. "That sounds divine."

"I'll pack a bottle of good wine, a chocolate dessert, and some fun toys."

"Toys?" she repeated, feigning innocence. "What kind of toys?"

"That'll be a surprise, but I think you'll enjoy them—eventually."

"What does that mean?"

"You'll find out."

"I wish we had a blanket right now. I wish we didn't have to worry about being seen. I wish our lives were normal, I wish—"

"Hey," he said, interrupting her, "keep the faith. Those wishes will all come true. I've got a plan cookin'. It needs to simmer, but I think it'll work."

"Oh, Luke, I do hope so."

"Is that the gate?" he asked, pointing ahead and asking Ghost to stop.

"Yes, that's it."

Continuing along the fence line, he halted next to it, and sliding off Ghost, she unhooked the halter and lead rope they'd attached to the saddle. Walking into the field, she stared across the open expanse for the small herd.

"Dusty," she called, her voice clear in the dark silence. "Come on, girl."

Tess heard Dusty's whinny and the cantering of hooves before she saw the stocky quarter horse gallop from the herd, her mane flying and her head tossing.

"She sure is happy to see you," Luke said with a chuckle as the mare stopped in front of Tess and nudged her.

"It's mutual," Tess replied, patting her mare's neck.

Sliding the halter over Dusty's head, she led her out of the field, making sure to securely latch the gate behind her.

"I need a minute to get this lead rope right," Tess muttered, looping the cord around Dusty's neck and attaching it to the halter on the opposite side.

Dusty remained perfectly still, and Luke admired Tess's calm, easy manner. It was obvious she was a natural horsewoman. Finally satisfied, with a graceful, almost balletic movement, she swung herself up on the horse's back.

"Damn, Tess, that was impressive."

"Really? Thanks. I've been doing it all my life."

"But I bet that's the first time it hurt when you landed."

Shooting him a look, with a cluck and a gentle kick, she sent her mare thundering forward. Thrilled to be ridden, the mare bucked and played as she took off across the field. Pushing his big gelding into a gallop to catch up, Luke couldn't help but admire Tess's ability. She had no saddle or stirrups, but she remained balanced and centered on Dusty's back in spite of the mare's frolicking.

"Hey, slow down," he called as he drew closer. "It's a long ride back. We need to pace ourselves."

Slowing Dusty to a trot, then a walk, Tess spun her head around and grinned back at him.

"It's not my fault if you can't keep up."

Falling into step next to her, Luke laughed out loud.

"Your mare is somethin' else. What a great little horse."

"She is, and she's really brave."

"Like her owner."

Swallowed up by an unexpected warm blush, and not sure what to say, Tess leaned forward and patted Dusty's neck. Luke saw it as another sign of the sweet, modest girl who lived inside the sometimes reckless, sometimes bratty, sometimes stubborn woman.

They were soon back at the hunting lodge and tacking up Ghost, but as they left, and rode up the gentle slope, Tess let out a wistful sigh.

"It was only one night, but it was a night I'll never forget," she murmured as they reached the top of the hill.

"Neither will I," he said, letting out a sigh. "Maybe once I've cleared my name, old man Anderson will let me rent it for a weekend."

"I'm sure he will. You worked for him forever. Didn't he step up as a character witness at your trial?"

"Yep. He was the only one. I was surprised. He made no secret about his wish for you and Tyler to get together, just like your dad. They had the two of you hitched the day you were born."

"I know, but it was never going to happen. Tyler wasn't my type, not even close. I didn't even like him much when we were kids."

"Is that so?" Luke said, tilting his head to the side. "Tell me, Tess, exactly what is your type?"

Glancing across at him, she smiled a sassy smile and winked.

"I think I'm just finding that out."

"You'll have to let me know when you do," he retorted, winking back at her.

"What's your type, Luke Larson?"

"Sassy, smart and sexy, just like you."

"Good answer," she quipped with a laugh.

They continued their late night journey chatting about everything from the weather, to the challenges of ranch life, then how disturbingly easy it had been for Luke to be arrested and convicted for a crime he'd had no part in.

"It makes me wonder how many others are behind bars who don't belong there," he remarked solemnly. "If it happened to me, it can happen to anyone."

"It's truly terrible," Tess murmured. "I'll do anything to make sure you're cleared."

"Thanks, Tess, but remember your promise."

"Don't worry, I will."

Finally reaching the top of the low hill that would drop them down to the back of Luke's ranch, he paused, staring out across the terrain in search of any unfamiliar vehicles that might be staking out his home. Seeing nothing out of place, he texted Robbie, alerting him they'd be at the back of the barn in a few minutes. Returning his phone to his pocket, Tess leaned across the space between them and touched his arm.

"Wait," she murmured, a catch in her voice.

"What is it?" he asked, worried she may have seen something in the shadows that he'd missed.

"I feel so—I don't know—sad," she whispered. "We're going back into the reality of the nightmare. You'll be chasing the culprit and hiding out at my house, and the whole town will be watching for you. I'm scared. The lodge was an escape. I felt as if no-one could hurt us there."

"Hey," he murmured, taking her hand and squeezing it tightly. "This will all work itself out."

"But you don't know that."

"Call me crazy, but somethin' inside me keeps tellin' me things are gonna be just fine. Call it instinct, a gut feelin', call it faith if you want, but I believe it, and I wouldn't be here if I didn't. Do I have doubts? Sure, a bunch, but they're not gonna stop me."

"Luke..."

Moving Ghost closer to Dusty and holding his reins in one hand, he brought the other to the back of her head, leaned across the narrow space between them, and pressed his lips against hers.

The lingering, loving kiss enveloped Tess in a tingling warmth. As their mouths mingled longingly, their tongues lightly touched, sending her pulse racing and her butterflies fluttering. His mouth was full and moist, his hand on the back of her head firm and sure, and when he pressed with greater fervor, his lips suddenly demanding, she moaned as an aching need surged through her sex.

"Damn, Tess," he breathed, breaking away, his fingers move into her hair. "You send my blood pumpin' like no other woman I ever met."

The intense blaze in his eyes, the grip of his hand, and the sparkling passion radiating from him, exposed the truth in his soul. With her heart thundering, she whispered,

"I love you too."

CHAPTER THIRTEEN

ROBBIE WAS STANDING next to Luke's 1970's Cadillac sedan when Luke and Tess arrived at the barn. As Luke removed his saddle, Tess led Dusty into a stall, then made sure there was plenty of hay and water for both horses.

"You'll be staying here for a little while," Tess said softly, petting her mare's neck, "but you'll have Ghost to keep you company."

"Don't worry," Robbie assured her. "I'll take good care of her."

"Thanks, Robbie. She's easy. Never worries about anything much, but she can have an attitude once and a while."

"I can't imagine where she gets that from," Luke remarked with a grin, leading Ghost into his stall.

"Very funny," Tess quipped, shooting him a look.

"But true!" he retorted, then taking her hand, they followed Robbie outside and climbed into the back seat of the classic car.

"It's a good thing you kept this old beauty," he declared as he settled behind the wheel.

"Every cowboy needs a getaway car," Luke replied with a grin. "It's in such great condition," Tess remarked. "This interior looks almost brand new. How long have you had it?"

"I guess about ten years. It was my dad's, and he's always been meticulous about his vehicles. I did my best to keep up his standards. He'd shoot me if I didn't. She's never given me any trouble, not that I've driven her much."

With Luke and Tess crouched low in the back seat, Robbie drove slowly down the drive and out the front gate, keeping his eyes peeled for hidden cars that might be watching the ranch.

"I don't see anything," he muttered as he headed down the desolate road, "and no-one's followin' us."

"Have you called Dwayne yet? Does he know we're comin'?" Luke asked.

"Not yet. I wanted to make sure we were gonna make it," Robbie replied. "No sense gettin' him all wired and ready if things don't work out the way we planned. I thought I'd call him after we drive around the block a couple of times."

"Good thinking," Luke murmured, "and what a blessing he popped up out of nowhere."

"My heart almost stopped when he approached me," Robbie said, glancing at Luke in the rearview mirror. "I honestly thought we were done for, but then he went into this long story about how he needed to do the right thing, just the way he did with you on the phone."

"Sometimes the simplest minds are the smartest," Tess piped up. "My brother and the sheriff can't see the forest for the trees!"

IN THE GUEST ROOM AT Tess's house, the melody of Sweet Home Alabama unexpectedly exploded through the air, jolting Dwayne from a sound sleep. Gasping from the shock, he stared at his phone, then hastily snatched it from the nightstand.

"Hello? Hello? This is Dwayne."

"Sorry to wake you, Dwayne, it's Robbie."

"Oh, uh, hi. Is everything all right?"

"Yes, just fine. I'm dropping off our two friends in the alley behind the house. Could you please unlock the back door and keep your dog quiet? We're about two minutes away, and Dwayne, don't turn on any lights."

"Huh? Oh, yeah, right, sure, no problem, I'll be there," he stammered, then ending the call, he wondered if he'd left any dishes in the sink. "No, I didn't," he muttered. "You hush up now, Rex," he continued, patting his big dog on the head and snapping the leash on his collar. "Don't go makin' any noise when they come in."

If Rex was on a leash he'd stay quiet. It was something Dwayne still didn't understand, but from the day he'd rescued the oversized mutt from the animal shelter, it was how the dog had behaved.

Quickly pulling on his jeans and a T-shirt, Dwayne moved quickly through the dark house to the kitchen. Telling Rex to sit, he turned the deadbolt, pushed open the door, and peered into the yard. Pricking his ears, Rex let out a low growl.

"Easy, boy."

His dog was telling him people were close by, and unfazed by Dwayne's command, he stood up and let out a whine.

"Shush," Dwayne whispered, tugging lightly on the leash.

Rex immediately sat down and looked up at him.

'Good boy,' Dwayne murmured softly, patting him. "They're friends." The latch on the gate clicked. Stepping into the yard dressed in the long, black sweater, Tess was barely visible. Luke followed, and quietly closing the gate behind him, he took her hand and they hurried across the lawn.

"Hey, Dwayne," Luke whispered as they approached. "You're a lifesaver. Thank you."

"Are you guys doin' okay?" Dwayne asked as they slipped past him and into the house. "Should I fix some coffee or somethin'? What can I do?"

"Dwayne, you've already done enough," Tess replied gratefully. "I don't know where we'd be without your help."

"I feel so bad about what happened to you, Luke," Dwayne muttered with a deep frown. "I had to do somethin'. It was only right."

"I love the way you think," Luke said with a grin. "Tess and I are both pretty tired. We're gonna hit the hay, but in the mornin' we'll figure out where to go from here, and you big guy," Luke grinned, staring down at the odd-looking, large dog, "you're a champion. You didn't make a peep when we walked up."

Rex tilted his head and whined, then lifted his paw.

"He's absolutely adorable," Tess said with a wide smile. "I want to get to know him, but Luke's right, we need to go to bed. I'm totally wiped out."

"I'll try to be real quiet in the mornin'," Dwayne said earnestly, "and Rex here, he won't make any noise unless I tell him it's okay."

"Not to worry," Luke assured him, continuing to pet the dog. "Goodnight, Rex, and goodnight to you too, Dwayne. Thanks again for all the help."

Dwayne watched them head off, but feeling uncomfortable at the thought of following them down the hall, he gave Rex a treat and waited until he heard the bedroom door close.

"They sure are nice people," he mumbled, leading his dog back to the guest room. "It's a good feelin' knowin' we're gonna make things right. I'd say it's just about the best feelin' in the whole world."

AFTER A QUICK SHOWER, Tess and Luke snuggled between the sheets, and though exhausted, their need for each other was stronger than their weariness. Instructing her not to make a sound, Luke sent his mouth to her neck, then lips, then hungrily devoured her nipples as his fingers toyed between her legs.

His stiffened cock rested against her thigh, and as she wrapped her fingers tightly around his shaft, he clenched his teeth to silence his groan. Abruptly kneeling up, he grabbed her ankles, lifted them in the air, pulled them wide apart, and touched the tip of his cock against her entrance. As she softly whimpered her need, he slid forward into her depths, then lowered his body on hers, and listening to her whispered moans, he rode her until they were crossing the finish line in sweet, orgasmic euphoria.

Moments later, lying in his arms and completely drained, Tess passed out with barely a murmur. Engulfed in their closeness, knowing he was safe for another passage of the moon, Luke sank into the mattress and drifted into a dreamless sleep.

ACROSS TOWN JEB WASN'T so lucky. Not wanting to wake his wife with his tossing and turning, he'd slipped from the bed and padded into the kitchen. Pouring himself a scotch, he plonked himself down at the breakfast table and took a much-needed swig.

"Damn you, Luke Larson. You either got away or you never left," he muttered under his breath. "You sure as hell weren't on that train when it pulled in Longville, and you weren't seen in those first three towns either, dang it! Four more to go, and if we draw a blank with them, then where the hell are you? There's no way you could jump off that train runnin' at full throttle." Taking another drink, his frown grew deeper.

"Hmm, kinda funny Tess got sick about the same time. I wonder... no, that has to be a coincidence. Dwayne's there, still, I think I'll knock on her door in the mornin'. I should see how she's doin' anyway." Gulping down the last of the scotch, he set the glass in the sink and wandered back to the bedroom. His wife, Glynis, rolled over to welcome him as he climbed back into bed.

"Is the hunt for Luke Larson troublin' you, hon?"

"Yep. I don't know where the blazes he's disappeared to," Jeb grunted, letting out a frustrated sigh.

"Do you want to know why I think he came back?"

"I sure would. It's got me stumped."

"I bet he's innocent. That's what innocent men do. They go back to where they were wronged and try to clear their names. Isn't that what you'd do if you were convicted of a crime you didn't commit?"

"How do you know he didn't do it?"

"Haven't you been listening? That's my theory. That's why he's come back. If he'd escaped to escape and was guilty, he'd be on the other side of the country. He sure as heck wouldn't come back here."

Jeb frowned at the ceiling, pondering his wife's words.

"Damn, you're right," he murmured. "That's exactly what I'd do."

"So—that tells you two things, he didn't do it, and he's still here."

Rolling on his side and raising himself up on his elbow, he stared down at his high-school sweetheart.

"You always were smarter than me."

"And let's not forget, better looking."

"That too," he replied with a grin, "but regardless, it's my job to find him and arrest him. What I think about his guilt or innocence doesn't matter."

"Sure it does," she exclaimed, "and you can be hunting for him and hunting for the truth at the same time. Open up the file. Take a look with fresh eyes. Maybe something will jump out at you, something you missed."

"I'm not a detective, Glyn."

"No, but there was a time you wanted to be," she reminded him, "and that Alex fella you like so much, don't you call him Sherlock behind his back? Get him on it as well."

"You know, maybe I will, and I'll tell the sheriff what you said first thing in the mornin'. It makes all the sense in the world. I should check on Tess too, see how she's doin'."

"You should, just don't bring back anything contagious, and those are my last wise words for the night," she declared, surrendering to a yawn, then closed her eyes and went back to sleep.

Flopping on his back, Jeb thought about the number of times he'd had doubts about Luke's guilt. He didn't know the man well, but everyone he'd interviewed who did, swore Luke was not a guy who'd push a girl to have sex, or attack an old man.

But the evidence had been overwhelming.

The weapon used to attack Nate, and the money that had been stolen, were found in Luke's garage hidden behind a stack of old crates.

"Patty Jamison," he muttered under his breath. "If I'm going to look at this again, that's where I need to start. I'll have a chat with her and take Alex along for the ride."

Pleased with his decision, he rolled over, and spooning his wife, he finally felt himself drift into sleep.

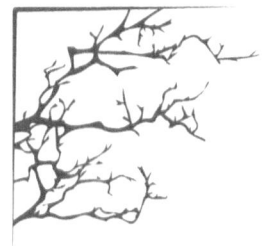

CHAPTER FOURTEEN

WAKING UP NEXT TO LUKE holding her from behind, Tess let out a groggy moan, pushed back against him, then winced.

"Ouch. Why does my butt still hurt?"

"Cos I spanked you good and proper," Luke murmured, his hands clasping her breasts as his mouth nuzzled her neck.

"Ooh, Luke, that feels so good." "Even with a sore backside?"

"Even with a sore backside," she softly repeated, "I'm so glad Dwayne went out early this morning."

"He probably figured we needed to be alone, at least for a while."

"Maybe he just had to walk Rex."

"Regardless, are you ready for me to fuck you senseless?" he whispered, snaking his way inside her.

"As long as you don't stop if he comes back."

"Ooh, you are such a wicked girl," he growled, plunging forward with gusto. Shifting back from her body, he moved his hands from her breasts to grip her hips, and as he began vigorously pumping, she buried her face in the pillow to stifle her cries. Determined to take her to the hilt without a single pause, he accelerated, slamming her sex with strong, swift strokes. When her moans grew louder, and her breathing came in short, sharp gasps, he slid a hand between her legs and urgently rubbed her clit.

"Luke," she panted, lifting her head, "I'm there!"

"Come for me, darlin, come for me now."

As she arched her back and let out a high pitched, euphoric wail, he exploded with a violent eruption, and in spite of his powerful convulsions he slipped his hand over her mouth to stifle her continuing howls.

But all too soon their spasms waned.

Collapsing on the bed, he rolled her over, and as he pulled her into his arms he heard her mumble something. "What did you say?" he asked breathlessly, willing his heart to stop it's thunderous pounding.

"I said," she gasped, "I didn't know sex could be like this. I feel as if I'm living a dream."

"I hope it stays a dream," he said softly, letting out a heavy breath, "and doesn't turn back into a nightmare."

"I'll run away with you if it looks like that's going to happen."

"That's not—"

But a loud banging on the front door made them both jump. Glancing at the clock, she let out a small cry of surprise.

"Holy crap, it's almost 10:30. I had no idea it was so late."

"I'm not surprised," he remarked. "We needed that sleep. You'd better see who it is."

Climbing quickly from the bed and grabbing her robe, she ran through the house to the front door, but when she peered through the peephole her heart skipped. It was Jeb. Doing her best to control the churning in her gut, she took a long, deep breath and told herself to stay calm.

"Hi, Jeb," she said, opening the door just enough to lean against the frame. "Sorry it took me a while. I was sleeping."

"At this time of day?"

"I'm still sick, or did you forget already?" she asked testily. "What's up? It's cold and I don't feel good. I need to go back to bed."

"I just wanted to check on you. Where's Dwayne?"

"I don't know. I guess he took Rex out. Like I said—I was asleep," she said pointedly.

"Glynis wanted to know if she could bring you anything, soup, food, whatever. Can I come in, or are you gonna keep me out here on the doorstep?"

"Jeb, sorry, but I need to lie down. Tell Glynis thanks, but I can't really stomach anything right now."

"Poor kid," he said, his voice softening. "Sorry, I feel bad I woke you up. Go and get some rest, I'll call you later."

"Uh, Jeb, is there any news about Luke Larson?" "Not yet. No-one has seen him, but we've got more checkin' to do. Glynis thinks he's still in town."

The knot in her stomach tightened.

"She does? Why is that?"

"She said an innocent man would come back to clear his name, and she's got a point," he remarked, a slight frown creasing his forehead. "I'm gonna open up the file and give it another read through."

"Good for you, Jeb. An open mind will never let you down, but I've gotta go. I'm starting to feel a bit dizzy."

"Get better, sis, and again, I'm sorry I got you outta bed."

"It's okay, I'm glad you care," she said with a half-smile. "Call me if you come up with anything."

"Sure. Catch ya, later."

"Bye, Jeb."

Quickly closing the door, she broke into a smile and hurried back to the bedroom.

"Who was it?" Luke asked as she dropped the robe and crawled back into bed.

"Jeb!"

"Jeb? Damn. How'd it go?"

"I'm so glad I was here. Glynis told him she thinks you're still in town because, and I quote, an innocent man would return to clear his name."

"Smart woman," he muttered. "Smarter than her husband."

"He actually listened. He's going to open the file and give it another read."

"Seriously?"

"That's what he said, and I know him. He can be like a dog with a bone. Glynis has started him thinking, and he won't be satisfied until he's sure he knows the truth."

"That's great news. Let's just hope he finds something." "And soon," Tess said earnestly. "I want you to get your life back. I want to walk through town holding your hand."

A sudden frown crossed her brow.

"Hey, it'll happen," he reassured her. "I guess seeing Jeb and being back here is suddenly hitting me. Hiding away at the lodge was like a romance novel, but now we're back in all the crap! What if you can't prove you didn't do it, what if...?"

Unable to finish, her brow crinkling, tears threatened. Nestling against him, she closed her eyes and sank into his powerful hold.

"Hey, Tess, your brother isn't the only one who's like a dog with a bone. I'm not gonna rest until I'm cleared," he said softly, "and don't forget what he said. I'm a crafty fella."

"I love you," she whispered, "more than you can know. I couldn't stand it if you were taken away."

"And I love you Tess. I'm not gonna let that happen."

"I was such an idiot to listen to everyone back then," she muttered. "You should spank me for that too."

"Shush now. People were yappin' in your ear all those months ago. You could have turned me in when I walked into the cafe the other night, but you didn't. You chose to help me. You knew in your heart I'd done nothin' wrong."

"You're right, I felt it the minute you looked at me." "Exactly. Now let's get ourselves up and have some breakfast. Dwayne will probably be back soon, and I'm sure he'll be hungry. You take a shower by yourself though, cos if I go in there with you, we'll end up right back here."

"I think you're right," she replied, shifting in his arms and staring up at him, then softly pressing her lips against his, she slipped from the bed.

Watching her pad into the bathroom, he sat up and stretched his arms above his head. No amount of wishful thinking would prove his innocence. That would take careful planning and staying focused—and luck. He needed the ball to bounce in his favor.

The sound of the back door signaled Dwayne's return.

Luke closed his eyes and thought about his plan. He'd lay it out over breakfast.

AFTER A FULL MEAL OF pancakes, eggs, bacon, and toast, Tess began piling the dishes on the counter ready to load them in the dishwasher.

"Tess, that was the best breakfast I've ever eaten," Dwayne declared. "I'm gonna start comin' to your cafe. You're a real good cook."

"Thanks, Dwayne, and you're welcome any time. I owe you a lifetime of dinners for what you've done for us."

"Don't worry about those dishes," Luke said. "I need to talk to you. I have an idea. Come back and sit with us."

"You mean, an idea like a plan?" she asked, returning to the table and dropping into a chair.

"Yep."

"I can't wait to hear it," Dwayne said excitedly.

"Dwayne, before I tell you what I have in mind, if you don't want to be involved I'll totally understand. Your career is at stake."

"Dang, I don't even like my career. I keep tellin' my uncle I wanna work at the animal shelter," Dwayne declared, petting Rex sitting happily beside him. "I don't know why he doesn't believe me, I tell him all the time."

"That's too bad," Luke replied, then turned to Tess and took her hand. "Darlin', you know how I feel about puttin' you in harm's way, and this isn't exactly doin' that, but I'm still not sure—"

"Don't even go there," she exclaimed, cutting him off. "I'll do anything, and I mean anything, to help you, and if you don't involve me I won't be happy. In fact, I'll be very upset."

"I wouldn't want that," Luke said with a chuckle.

"Tell us," Dwayne said impatiently, "I'm dyin' to hear."

"Dwayne, I'm truly grateful, but I don't know what I did to deserve such loyalty. You barely know me."

"You're an innocent man! It's a bad thing that you were sent away. I may not like bein' a deputy, but I still want to do the best job I can. The other deputies think all they should do is catch you, but that's not true. It's catchin' the person who hurt Nate and robbed him that matters. If they took a minute to listen to you, *really* listen to you, they'd get that, but they won't, so it's up to me. Uh—did I say all that the right way?"

"You said it perfectly," Tess said, touching his arm, "and you're much smarter than they are."

"I am?"

"You bet," Luke said solemnly. "Much smarter, and you have a bigger heart."

"Aw, thanks," Dwayne muttered, his face blushing red. "Nobody's ever said anything like that to me before."

"I meant it."

"So did I," Tess said softly, then looked across the table at Luke. "Now will you tell us about this plan of yours?"

"Yep. Listen up..."

CHAPTER FIFTEEN

PATTY JAMISON HUMMED happily as she brushed her hair and checked her reflection in the mirror. Every Friday night she went to Barry's Bar, a festive place that offered a live country and western band, half-price drinks, and a wide selection of free munchies. She had yet to meet her dream man, but she was sure when she did it would be at Barry's.

Once upon a time she thought she had. Luke Larson, a rugged, handsome cowboy who'd put her over his knee and playfully spanked her until she'd squirmed so much she'd almost fallen off. Though she'd been shocked and embarrassed, she'd been totally turned on, and the sex afterwards had been nothing short of an exploding box of dynamite.

She often thought about that time, but with anger, not joy.

He'd ripped out her heart and stomped all over it.

When his presence in her head became too much, she carried out a ritual to exorcise him. It had happened several times over the last few days. News traveled quickly in the small community, and she'd heard he was on the loose.

Donning a dark green shirt and black jeans, she pulled on her black cowboy boots, grabbed her favorite suede jacket with the fringe, and checked her purse to make sure she had her can of mace. Picking it up, a dark frown crossed her face.

"I'll happily spray you if you cross my path, you bastard," she muttered, lifting it out. "Nothing would give me greater pleasure."

Letting out a sigh and dropping it back in her bag, she started out the door. Her cabin didn't have an attached garage, and as she trotted down the porch steps to the carport, she paused. It was an out of the way spot, which was one of the reasons she'd rented it, but since hearing of Luke's escape she'd been particularly aware.

Standing in the growing darkness, her senses were in high alert.

Finally satisfied, she continued down to her car and headed off.

ON TOP OF A RIDGE, a ten minute ride away, Luke was sitting on Ghost, peering through his small, but powerful binoculars. Barry's Bar was where he'd first hooked up with Patty Jamison, and thanks to Dwayne, he'd learned her habits hadn't changed. After watching the red tail lights of her car disappear into the night, he moved Ghost slowly forward and followed the track down to the cabin.

WHEN PATTY WALKED INTO the bar, the band was playing up a storm. Couples danced, others clapped along to the music, and sitting at several tables pushed together, a raucous group laughed out loud. Buoyed by the upbeat crowd she moved to the bar and perched herself up on her favorite stool. It was towards the end, offering a view of the stage and the dance floor, but far enough away to carry on a conversation with Daniel, the handsome bartender. "What'll it be?" he asked, sauntering up to her.

"I'm glad Barry hired you," she replied flirtatiously. "I look forward to coming here even more now."

"Thanks, Patty," he said with a grin. "I'm always happy to see you too."

"I'll have a Margarita with a basket of chips and that great salsa?"

"You got it."

Admiring his tall, wide-shouldered frame, she decided it was time to ask him over to her cabin. She hadn't had sex in far too long, and he was about as hunky as they came.

"Try not to worry," a male voice said from behind her. "Luke is as good as caught. He can't stay in hiding forever."

Turning around to see who had made the comment, she was surprised to spot Tess Turner sitting at a table with a young man who looked vaguely familiar.

"I hope you're right, Dwayne," Tess replied. "It sickens me that he's out. I hate that man with every fibre of my being."

Patty pricked her ears.

Dwayne.

He was a dullard, but he was also the sheriff's nephew.

He'd be in the loop.

"I don't blame you," Dwayne replied. "That man turned out to be a real bad dude. Shoot, my phone, hang on a sec, Tess."

Watching him answer his call, Patty saw an annoyed expression cross his face.

"Yep, okay," he said, then quickly dropped his phone back into his pocket. "Sorry, Tess, my brother's dang car won't start and I've gotta go help him. Do you wanna leave or wait for me?"

"It's early, and it feels good to be out. I'll stay here and people watch."

"Okay, I'll be back soon," he promised, and grabbing his jacket off the back of his chair, he hurried out the door.

"Here you go, Patty," the bartender said, placing her drink and snack in front of her. "Do you want to start a tab?"

Turning back to the bar, she gazed at the boyish grin of the super cute man smiling at her.

"Yeah, and do you know what that woman over there is drinking?"

"That is my specialty Mai Tai," he replied, staring across at Tess. "Whip one up and I'll take it over."

FROM THE CORNER OF her eye, Tess nervously watched Patty Jamison approach the table.

The plan had sounded simple enough.

Run into Patty and get her talking about that fateful night.

Suddenly it didn't seem simple at all.

"Hi, I'm Patty Jamison. You're Tess Turner right?" "That's me," Tess replied, lifting her eyes.

"I'm not sure if you know who I am, but—"

"Patty? Of course I know you who you are."

"May I join you? I bought you a Mai Tai. That's what you're drinking, right?"

"That's very kind of you. Please, sit down. Your timing is perfect, and what a coincidence," Tess said earnestly, wishing her heart would settle. "I was just talking with my friend about Luke Larson and what a bastard he is. I can't believe he's out on the streets."

"You really think he's a bastard?"

"Don't you?" Tess said, hoping she hadn't broached the subject too soon.

"Totally."

"I, uh, I don't mean to pry," Tess continued, lowering her voice, "but I heard he wouldn't take no for an answer. Is that true?"

"I'm afraid it is," Patty replied, leaning across the table, "but I managed to fight him off."

"Wow, you're so lucky you got away," Tess murmured, engaging the girl's eyes. "I propose a toast! To the cops catching Luke Larson sooner rather than later."

"Absolutely."

They clinked glasses, but while Tess took a sip, Patty downed a large swallow of her margarita.

"You left this behind," the handsome bartender declared, suddenly appearing at the side of the table with the untouched basket of tortilla chips and a bowl of salsa.

"Thanks, Daniel," Patty said, smiling up at him. "This is Tess. Keep the drinks and munchies coming. Tess and I have a lot to talk about."

"Will do."

"How hunky is he?" Patty whispered as he walked away.

"Super hunky," Tess agreed, though she found the bartender too slick for her taste.

"I'm going to ask him over to my cabin."

"Isn't that risky? You don't really know him, do you?" "Not really, but that's half the fun. Taking risks keeps life exciting, and I haven't had much excitement lately."

"That sounds like another toast," Tess exclaimed. "Here's to taking risks."

"Taking risks," Patty repeated, raising her glass and taking a swallow.

Tess sipped and smiled.

Luke had been right.

Getting Patty Jamison plastered and talking up a storm wouldn't be difficult at all.

WITH GHOST TIED UP in a nearby thicket, Luke had crept to the cabin and peeked through the windows. A small lamp burned by a couch, and from what he could see, nothing in the living room had changed since he'd been there. Moving around to the back door, he checked under a row of flowerpots, finding the key on the third try. Smiling as he recalled the old adage, third time lucky, he unlocked the back door, and was about to enter, but paused. Not wanting to trip over anything, he retrieved his powerful flashlight and sent the bright beam across the floor.

"What the hell is that," he muttered, crouching down.

His heart skipped.

Three trip wires had been strung across the threshold. Shining his light across the kitchen, his heart leapt a second time. Several boards with four inch nails sticking straight up sat below the kitchen window.

Grateful for his natural caution, he straightened up, stepped over the wires, and made his way around the deadly boards. With the light illuminating his path, he moved cautiously forward. Patty had told him about a collection of diaries kept in several shoe boxes locked in the hall closet. She had even boasted they would become a best-selling book one day. Though the hall appeared to be clear, he stopped to take a breath. The closet was only a few yards ahead, but he'd broken out in a sweat and his nerves were on edge.

"Easy, boy," he muttered under his breath. "Just stay calm and focused." Moving slowly forward and reaching the door, he shone the flashlight around the frame looking for anything out of the ordinary. It wasn't until he studied the doorknob he saw it. A tiny wire wrapped around its base.

White tape made it barely discernible against the white of the door, then it disappeared into the narrow gap where the door met the frame. Dropping to his knees and carefully pulling back the rug, he found the wire continued beneath it, leading to a plug in a power socket.

"The damn thing is set to electrocute someone," he breathed, a shudder rippling through him as he pulled the plug from the point. "What the hell is so important?"

Moving back to the closet and doing one last check around the door, he took a deep breath, slowly turned the handle and opened it.

His blood ran cold.

The boxes were gone, but plastered across the walls were pictures of him, newspaper clippings, pieces of paper with his name scrawled across it, and in the center, a blow up of a photograph taken of the two of them at a party. She had scratched out his eyes and drawn a dagger through his heart. It took a moment, but the dawning realization took hold.

"No-one put you up to luring me out to the lake!" he breathed, his heart pounding a mile a minute. "You were acting alone. You hit poor Nate, and you stashed the money and my crowbar in my garage." Quickly grabbing his phone, he photographed the horrifying shrine, making sure he shot from every angle. With so many items pasted across the walls, some on top of others, he wanted to make sure he didn't miss anything. Finally finished, he carefully closed the door and took photographs of the wire around the handle, and after putting the plug back into the point, he took a picture of that as well. Shaking his head, he stared back at the innocent looking closet, then cautiously made his way back through the house.

Safely outside, he placed the key back in its hiding place, but as he hurriedly returned to Ghost, he had a sudden flash of panic.

"Damn! Tess! You're with that nut job." Urgently pulling out his phone to text Dwayne, he discovered he had no signal. Jumping quickly on Ghost he trotted up the hill, and as they zigzagged down the other side, Luke finally found a place from which he could call.

"Hi, Luke, is everything okay?" Dwayne asked

"It is on this end, but I need you to make sure Tess doesn't go any-where with Patty," Luke said urgently. "I'll explain later, but go back and get Tess away from her. Make up some excuse."

"Uh, like what?"

"Where did you say you were going?"

"To help my brother with his car," Dwayne answered, "not that I have a brother."

"Tell her you stopped by the house to check on Rex and he was gone, and you need her help to find him."

"But Rex would never—"

"Tess and Patty won't know that," Luke said hastily, cutting him off.

"Oh, good point. I'll go back to Barry's right away, and see you back home."

Ending the call, Luke headed for his ranch. It hadn't been an easy ride to get to Patty's cabin, but it had been well worth the effort. "I suppose I should've hunted for those boxes," he muttered, as Ghost moved down the hill, "but you probably have them hidden away with more booby traps. I was lucky to get in and out of your house in one piece as it is."

WHEN DWAYNE ARRIVED at Barry's Bar, Luke's suggestion wasn't sitting well. If Rex had gone missing, he wouldn't have driven all the way back to the bar to fetch Tess. He would have called and told her he was roaming the streets looking for him.

Leaning against his car and staring at the ground, he tapped his foot as he hummed a song, thinking about how he'd enjoyed the last couple of days hanging out at Tess's house, how he'd managed to fool Jeb, how—

"That's it," he exclaimed loudly.

Grabbing his phone, he texted Jeb.

At Barry's Bar with Tess, having a great time. You and Glynis should join us.

He waited impatiently, staring at his screen, then broke into a broad smile.

On our way.

As he ambled back to the bar, a Cheshire Cat grin on his face, he decided maybe he wasn't such a dummy after all.

"People think I am, I know that," he muttered, "but sometimes it just takes me a while."

CHAPTER SIXTEEN

TESS STARED IN DISBELIEF as Jeb and Glynis waved at her from the door of the tavern and began walking to her table. She was already annoyed Dwayne had returned early.

"Hey, Tess, isn't that your brother?" Patty asked. "I've never seen him out of uniform."

"Yes, that's my brother," Tess replied, wondering what the blazes he was doing there.

"Hi, Jeb, hi, Glynis," Dwayne said as they approached. "It's good to see you guys."

"Patty, what a coincidence," Jeb remarked. "I won't talk shop now, but if you're gonna be around tomorrow I'd like to stop by for a quick word."

"Sure. What about?"

"What happened with Larson," Jeb answered casually. "I'm giving the file a review."

Tess could feel her head beginning to spin. Though she wasn't sure how many drinks she'd had, she realized it was one too many.

"Tess, how are you feeling?" Jeb asked as he and Glynis sat down. "I'm surprised you're out. Do you think it's a good idea after being sick for the last couple of days?"

"I started feeling better this afternoon, and I wanted to take Dwayne out for a drink to thank him for being my bodyguard."

"Tess, I hate to be a party pooper," Dwayne interjected, "but your brother might be right. Maybe we should get you home. You don't want to relapse."

"That's very thoughtful Dwayne," she replied, still wondering why he'd returned sooner than he should have.

"I know we just got here," Glynis said sweetly, "but I have to agree with Jeb and Dwayne. If you just got out of bed, you don't want to over-do it."

"Don't forget, Tess," Dwayne announced, leaning across the table and staring at her intently, "I have to walk Rex, and if I don't get back soon he'll start barking."

She paused.

Dwayne wanted her to leave.

"You're probably right," she replied with a resigned sigh. "Sorry, Patty, I was really enjoying our visit. Maybe we can get together again soon."

"Yeah, let's do that," Patty agreed. "I don't have many friends here."

"Make sure you get straight to bed," Jeb said firmly as Tess rose to her feet.

"I have to admit I am starting to feel a bit knackered, but I'm glad I ran into you both. I'd hug you but—"

"No thanks," Glynis said with a grin. "We don't need to get the bug."

As Tess followed Dwayne through the bar and out to the parking lot, though she was dying of curiosity, she waited until they were safely in the car.

"Dwayne, what's going on?"

"This is kinda heavy," he began as he drove from the parking lot. "Luke called and said to make sure you weren't alone with Patty, and told me to get you away from her. I texted Jeb hoping he'd come over and kinda, you know, disrupt things so I could get you out, and he did."

"That was really smart, Dwayne. Thank you!"

"You think so? Thanks. I figured friends walkin' in like that wouldn't seem suspicious. Did Patty say anything important?"

"Not specifically, but she sure doesn't like Luke. I'll call her tomorrow and arrange another night out."

"Uh, I don't think he'll want you to do that," Dwayne said solemnly. "He must have found somethin' bad at her house."

"I hope he's home, and I wish we could get Jeb out of town again. It's a lot of pressure having him around, especially now Luke's at my house."

"I imagine so," Dwayne murmured, swinging his car into Tess's driveway and parking behind the garage.

As they ambled to the front door, they were welcomed by Rex's loud bark, and walking inside, Tess called Luke's name, but received no response.

"I guess he's not here," she remarked. "Do you want some coffee while we wait?"

"No thanks, I'm gonna take Rex for a walk. I won't be long."

Hearing the word *walk,* Rex whined and wagged his tail, making Tess laugh out loud. Grabbing the leash off the coat rack, Dwayne attached it to the dog's collar.

"Come on, fella, let's go."

After watching them head out, she was hanging her coat on the hall tree when she heard the sound of the back door. Hurrying into the kitchen she found Luke closing it behind him.

"Thank goodness you're home safe," she declared, hurrying across and hugging him tightly. "Why didn't you want me alone with Patty?"

"Just let me hold you for a second," he murmured, wrapping her up.

"Luke, what is it?"

"Best sit down, hon," he said gravely, "there's something I have to show you."

WALKING HIS DOG AROUND the block, Dwayne pondered Tess's words.

I wish we could get Jeb out of town again. It's a lot of pressure having him around.

He had to agree. It was nerve-racking having the Deputy Sheriff constantly on the prowl, and Dwayne could imagine how difficult it was for Tess and Luke. Walking up the path to the front porch, he unlocked the door and let himself in. Unsnapping Rex's leash, he could hear voices coming from the kitchen.

"And that's the problem, Tess. Other than emailing the pictures from some obscure computer, or printing them out and sending them, I don't know how to get them to Jeb?"

"I see what you mean, but there must be a way," Dwayne heard Tess reply.

As Rex suddenly bounded down the hall towards the kitchen, Dwayne quickly followed, finding Tess and Luke at the table.

"Hey, boy," she said with a grin. "Did you have a good walk?"

The large dog whined and lifted his paw, then dropped his head on her lap.

"Dwayne, I'm glad you're back," Luke declared. "Sit down and I'll fill you in."

"Yeah, I'm curious. What did you find at Patty's?"

"A bizarre shrine, unfortunately dedicated to me. It was locked in a booby-trapped closet," Luke said, handing Dwayne his phone. "If I hadn't spotted the wiring I would've been electrocuted. Check it out."

"Dang," Dwayne muttered, scrolling through the photographs. "This lady's plumb crazy!"

"Yep, but how can I get all those pictures to Jeb? There might be more information in her house that could clear me. I didn't stick around. Her back door and kitchen were booby-trapped too."

"Really? Huh. Weird. Hey, Luke, this is your burner phone, right?"

"Yep."

"I have an idea," Dwayne began. "Disguise yourself, hop that train to Longville, and text the photos to Jeb when you get there. He'll locate the signal and head up there to find you again."

"Holy crap, Dwayne, that's brilliant," Tess exclaimed. "Jeb will be gone and the pictures will be with the sheriff."

"But leave the phone in a taxi or a bus, so it looks like you're on the move."

"This just gets better and better," Tess said happily. "Dwayne, you're amazing. What do you think, Luke?"

"I'm embarrassed I didn't think of it myself," Luke replied with a grin, "but what can I do about a disguise?"

"I have some stuff from when I was in the Thanksgiving Day play," Dwayne said eagerly. "I was an old hobo, ragged clothes, beard, long grey hair, the whole bit."

"That's perfect!" Luke proclaimed. "Go home tonight, and bring everything back with you early in the morning. I'll change, and you can drop me at the woods near the station."

"You're going to get free meals forever!" Tess said gratefully.

"Aw, Tess, you folks are so nice. I'm just glad I was able to help."

A SHORT TIME LATER, Tess waved goodbye to Dwayne and Rex. Happy to have the house to themselves, she and Luke walked arm-in-arm to the bedroom and crawled into bed.

"Too many cocktails," she muttered, snuggling against him and letting out a heavy yawn.

"Make sure you're not alone with that crazy ass woman again. There's no tellin' what she might do."

"But Luke, you were right. I'm sure I could get her to open up to me."

"Dammit! Tess, what did I just say?"

"She can't do anything to me at Barry's Bar surrounded by people."

Abruptly sitting up, he grabbed her wrist and yanked her over his lap.

"Luke, stop, okay. You don't have to spank me!"

"Yep, I do," he said sternly, pushing the bed covers out of the way. "I'm not foolin' around with this," he declared, landing a hard swat. "If I have to make my point by burning your butt again, that's what I'll do. This is not open for debate, and if you have a tender behind while I'm in Longville, it'll remind you to do as you're told."

"I will," she promised, wriggling on his lap.

"You bet you will," he exclaimed, increasing the force and speed of his spanking hand, "and don't tell me to stop cos that'll only make me spank you harder."

Burying her head in the mattress, she squirmed as his hot palm delivered his message. When he finally stopped, though he'd smacked her for only a few minutes, he'd left her with a stinging behind.

"Have I made myself clear?"

"Yes, Sir," she whimpered. "I won't have anything to do with her."

"Thank goodness," he said softly, moving his hand across her scarlet bottom, then rolling her on her back, he pressed his fingers into her pussy.

"You're drippin'," he purred. "Do you want me to slide inside you?"

"Oh, Luke, you know I do."

Moving on top of her, he pinned her wrists on either side of her head, slowly pushed inside her, then pressed his lips on hers in an all-consuming kiss. As their mouths hungrily danced, he closed his eyes and lost himself in her soft cries, letting them guide his vigorous thrusting, holding her at bay several times, before pummeling her pussy, and sending her into her release.

AT HER CABIN, PATTY Jamison was busy removing her back door trip wires and bed of nails. She had told Daniel she needed to turn off the burglar alarm, and that's exactly what she was doing. She couldn't afford the regular type of security system, and she considered hers far more effective anyway. Hiding the nail boards under the sink, and winding back the trip wire, she hurried to her bedroom, turned on the bedside lamp, then moved quickly to the front door and waved for him to enter.

"This is a really cute place," Daniel remarked as he entered.

"Thanks. I love the privacy."

"What do you do, Patty?" he asked, taking her hand and pulling her onto the couch with him.

"I have a few investments," she replied vaguely, "but what about you? I've only seen you at Barry's for a couple of months. Where are you from?"

"I was working in corporate finance in New York, but I got tired of the crowds and noise, so I decided to take a couple of years and work my way through this great country."

"Wow, how fun."

"Now that's out of the way, why am I here? I get the feeling there's more to this invitation than a roll in the hay."

"You're right," she said coyly. "It's something kinky."

"I'm good with kinky. Very good. What did you have in mind?"

"Well...a while back...I went out with this guy who, uh, spanked me, and I really liked it."

"I'm definitely up for that, but I'll spank you hard. Very hard."

"Why?"

"A lovely woman I once knew, told me that there's nothing more frustrating than a spanking that's not hard enough. Would you agree with that?"

"I don't really know. Like I said, it's only happened once."

"Looking back, did you want this person to spank you more, or less?"

"If he'd spanked me less, it might not have felt the same. I don't just mean physically, I mean the whole thing."

"There, you see, you just answered the question, but I also spank hard because it's what I do, and I like spanking sitting on a bed. That way I can fuck your brains out as soon as I'm finished."

"Cool," she said, taking his hand and rising to her feet.

Leading him down the hall into her room, she reached to turn off the beside lamp, but he grabbed her wrist.

"No! I want to see your red behind, and I'll stay dressed, but you'll be naked," he said firmly. "If you want me to spank you, that's how it has to be."

"Wow, you really take charge."

"Yes, I do," he said sternly, climbing on the bed and leaning back against the headboard, "and Patty, don't make me wait."

She felt a small chill, but ignoring it, she quickly stripped, then waited for further instructions.

"Over my lap."

Taking a deep breath, she crawled across his thighs.

"Are you ready?" he asked, resting his hand on her backside.

"I sure am," she replied with a giggle.

"Now your ass is mine."

Placing one hand firmly on her waist, he raised the other and brought it down with a stinging smack, then continued with sharp, swift slaps.

"Stop," she suddenly howled, throwing her hand behind her.

Wordlessly grabbing her wrist, he thrust it up her back and re-sumed the spanking with vigorous abandon, swatting her bottom re-lentlessly, adding a finale of rapid-fire swats that had her wailing for mercy.

"I think that's good for now," he declared, squeezing her red skin.

"Fuck! You weren't kidding," she shrieked. "That was fucking hard."

"You can get up now."

Slowly sliding off his lap and rising to her knees, she rubbed her scorched skin.

"My ass is on fire."

"That sounded like a complaint."

"It was!"

"In that case," he said casually, moving from the bed, "I'll see you around."

"What? Wait, no, please don't leave."

"You've got a lot to learn," he said gravely. "I'll be tending bar at Barry's for the next few nights. If you decide to treat me with the re-spect I demand, and if you ask me nicely, and I mean really nicely, I might consider coming back here, otherwise, it's been interesting meet-ing you."

Stunned, she watched him walk away, then hurried after him, but saw only his back as he marched through the living room and strode outside to his car. A blast of cold night air swirled around her.

"What the fuck was that?" she muttered, hurrying to close the door, then shaking her head, she moved to the bathroom to stare at her red backside.

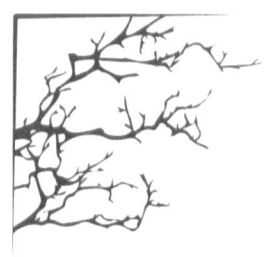

CHAPTER SEVENTEEN

EARLY THE FOLLOWING morning, Dwayne arrived at Tess's house with the costume he'd worn in the Thanksgiving Day play. After joining Tess and Luke for breakfast, they moved into the guest room, where Dwayne and Tess began transforming Luke into a homeless, elderly man. With Tess's make up skills, his skin became weathered and worn. The wig and beard followed, then dressing him in the raggedy clothes, the impossible was achieved. Luke Larson bore no resemblance to Luke Larson.

"This is amazing," Tess beamed, looking him up and down as she circled him. "If I ran into you on the street I'd never recognize you."

"I don't recognize myself," he said with a chuckle, staring at his reflection in the full length mirror. "I just hope I can get through all those trees and bushes without messing it up."

"You don't have to worry about that. Any more rips will only make it look more authentic," Tess remarked, then glanced at her watch. "We still have time for a second cup of coffee if you want one."

"Good, I need it. Sounds crazy, but I'm worn out from you two dressing me like this. Could you rustle that up for me, and maybe a muffin? I'll join you in a second. I want to see if I can find a way to wear these glasses and still see where I'm going."

"I had trouble with that too," Dwayne declared. "Here, I'll show you what I did."

"You go ahead, Tess. We'll only be a minute."

"Okay. It will be brewing," she said with a smile, and leaving him with Dwayne, she headed down the hallway towards the kitchen.

"You sure look different," Dwayne murmured. "Tess is right. I wouldn't recognize you either. About the glasses, I just sat them halfway down my nose and looked over them."

"Like this?" Luke asked, shifting them down.

"Yep, that's it," Dwayne replied.

"Perfect. What a blessing you were able to dig out this costume. Once again I must say thank you."

"I'm just glad I didn't throw it away," Dwayne said earnestly. "I had this funny feelin' I might need it."

"And you were right. By the way, do you know if Jeb will put you back on the roster now Tess is goin' back to work?"

"Yeah, he probably will. I expect he'll call me today, but I'm not sure if he wants me livin' back at my place yet. He likes Tess havin' Rex and me around."

"If you're available, would you please keep a sharp on her at the cafe tonight? I've persuaded her not to spend any time with Patty Jamison, but there's nothing I can do to stop Patty showing up at the restaurant. Tess being Tess, she wouldn't feel comfortable asking her to leave. I'd feel better if I knew you were watching over her. "

"I'm worried too," Dwayne agreed, a worried frown crossing his forehead. "Patty's a crazy woman. God Forbid Tess throws her out and makes Patty mad. There's no tellin' what might happen. You can leave it with me, Luke. Whether I'm on patrol or not, I'll keep swingin' by there, and I'll have dinner there as well."

"Dwayne, that's great. Be there at closin' time if you can. If Patty does show up, make sure she doesn't lure Tess away someplace for an after work drink. But we should go into the kitchen and join her. I'm dying' for that coffee."

"I'm about ready for another cup myself."

Placing the tinted spectacles in the breast pocket of the old, worn jacket, they left the bedroom and made their way to the kitchen.

"I had an idea," Tess announced as they entered, holding up a bottle of whiskey.

"A bit early in the day for that, don't you think?" Luke asked with a grin.

"Very funny, Luke Larson. I brought this out because you don't smell right. You need a sprinkle of whisky cologne."

"That's a good idea," Dwayne said eagerly. "Most of the bums I run across smell like they've been drinkin'—and they usually have."

"Please, not too much," Luke said, holding up his hands. "I have to live with it all day."

"Nope, just enough to tell the tale of drinks gone by."

Pouring a generous amount on a cloth, she wiped it across the front and back of his jacket.

"There, that's the finishing touch," she declared, then with a sigh, her face turned solemn. "I don't know how I'm going to work tonight, let alone sleep. I'll be so worried."

"Hey, darlin', this is a piece of cake," Luke assured her, "and once Jeb sees those photographs he'll know Patty set me up, or at least have a strong suspicion."

"I just wish there was more evidence," Tess continued, pouring the freshly brewed coffee into mugs and placing them on the table. "Help yourself to the sugar and cream."

"Thanks, Tess," Dwayne said gratefully as he sat down, "and you're right about that. Jeb and the sheriff keep tellin' us to focus only on cold, hard facts, not our theories."

"Then we need something that links Patty to Nate's assault," Tess declared. "But how will we get it?"

"The evidence will be there. Your brother just has to make the effort to look," Luke muttered, joining Dwayne at the table to drink his coffee. "Hopefully the photographs will motivate him to do that. Hey, Tess, you know not to go after it yourself, right?"

"Yes, Luke! You made that clear, and believe me, I got the message, but how can you be so sure there's something to be found? It's been so long."

"Forensics! What you see on TV, that's all real," Dwayne interjected. "Those little fibers and bits of skin and hair, they hang around like a bad smell. That's what Alex says, and he knows about that stuff. He wants to be a detective."

"Dwayne, you always know the right thing to say," she said reaching out and touching his arm. "Getting to know you has been the silver lining of this whole mess."

"I second that," Luke piped up.

"I-uh..." Dwayne stammered, his cheeks turning red. "It's been real nice gettin' to know the two of you as well."

"Shoot, I forgot to slice the walnut loaf," Tess declared, attempting to relieve the young man's embarrassment. "Would you like a piece to go with your coffee?"

"For sure," he nodded enthusiastically. "Hey, Rex? You want a nibble of walnut bread?"

Lying in the corner of the kitchen, the big dog stretched as he got to his feet, then padded across to the table.

"I'll take one too," Luke said with a grin, "and a piece to take with me if you can spare it."

"I'm already doing it, and I'll see what else I can put together for you," Tess promised, moving a knife through the rich, moist loaf.

A smile crossed her lips. She liked having a tender backside, and waking with Luke's muscled arms wrapped around her had been divine. Sitting across from him at breakfast felt natural, and Dwayne's unwavering loyalty during such a turbulent time had warmed her heart.

While the men finished their snack, she prepared a plastic tub with sandwiches, two slices of the walnut loaf, and two blueberry muffins, then placed it in the battered bag Dwayne had brought with the costume.

A SHORT TIME LATER, Luke climbed into the back seat of Tess's car, and as he laid on the floor, she tossed a blanket over him, just as she had the night he'd walked into the cafe and back into her life.

"This is becoming a habit," he declared.

"At least you're not locked up," Tess replied as she and Dwayne climbed into the front seat.

"This is true," he said, his voice muffled. "I'll take this over a prison cell any day."

Rolling down the driveway and onto the street, she drove several blocks, then turned down main street.

"Hey, there's your brother," Dwayne exclaimed, pointing squad car headed towards them on the opposite side of the road, "and that's Alex with him."

As they passed, Jeb shot her a big smile and waved.

"Now my phone will ring," Tess declared. "Five, four, three, two, one..."

As she'd predicted, the screen on her dashboard announced an incoming call and identified Jeb's name.

"Before you ask I'm just running some errands," she announced the moment she accepted the call.

"I'm glad you've got Dwayne with you, and Dwayne, thanks for looking out for my sister."

"It's my pleasure," Dwayne replied. "I haven't eaten this well since I left home."

"Where are you guys going?" Tess asked, wanting to make sure they weren't going near the train station.

"We're off to have a chat with Patty Jamison. While I'm talkin' to her, Alex will have a casual look around."

"Good for you. Will you let me know if she offers anything new, or if she has any changes in her story."

"Yeah, sure. The truth is, I've had a strange feelin' about that girl ever since she moved into town. I believed her when she said Luke had tried to force himself on her, but lookin' back maybe I was hasty. I mean, Luke kept to himself, but I never saw him as an unsavory character. When we found that evidence in his garage I just figured he was a dark horse. It was tough to explain that away. Still is."

Taking her eyes off the road, she rolled them upwards in frustration. One word from Glynis and he was having doubts, but at the time of Luke's arrest, Jeb had told her Luke Larson was guilty as sin, and it was a slam dunk case. Now listening to her brother, Tess didn't know whether to be relieved or furious.

"Tess, are you there?" he asked.

"Yes, I'm here, sorry, I'm just concentrating on turning into the lumber yard parking lot," she lied. "Keep me posted. I'm going now. Bye."

Ending the call, she shook her head.

"Unbelievable," she breathed. "Absolutely unbelievable."

"Did I just hear there's a light at the end of the tunnel?" Luke asked, moving the blanket away from his face.

"I don't know, maybe," Tess replied. "He was with Alex, and they're both going to see Patty. That's a good sign."

"It's certainly interesting. Dwayne, do you have a direct phone number for Alex? I wanna send him the photos as well."

"That's a good idea. I'll text it to you right now."

"Dammit, I wish they'd dug deeper when it all happened," Tess grumbled, "and I wish I'd had more time with Patty last night."

"Remember what I said about Patty," Luke warned. "Stay away from her."

"Luke's right," Dwayne said. "That woman is one crazy bitch."

"I know, I know," Tess replied impatiently, shifting in her seat, knowing what would happen if she chose to ignore Luke's warning, but it occurred to her she could have a long natter with her on the phone.

"I can hear the cogs in your brain turning, Tess," Luke exclaimed. "Dwayne's gonna be keepin' an eye out until I get back, so don't you go tryin' to track her down after work tonight."

"Don't worry, I won't," she promised, *thinking, at least not in person.*

CHAPTER EIGHTEEN

JEB AND ALEX HAD CALLED Patty to make sure she'd be home. When she answered the door and led them into the dining area off the lounge, they found coffee and cookies laid out on the table.

"Have a seat, and help yourselves. I baked the shortbread yesterday," she said proudly, "and the coffee is Kona. Do you like Kona?"

"Sure," Jeb replied as he sat down. "Thanks, Patty."

"I appreciate it, but I'll pass," Alex said, still on his feet. "I'm coffee'd out."

"So how can I help?" Patty asked, dropping into a chair opposite Jeb. "I told you everything all those months ago when it happened, so I'm not sure there's anything to add."

"I just want to go over your statement" Jeb replied. "As best as you can remember, could you please tell me the events of that night one more time?"

Standing off to the side, Alex listened as Patty began to recount her story, but his eyes scanned his surroundings. He had a unique ability to catch things that were out of place, and an instinct so keen, some of his fellow officers claimed he bordered on being psychic.

Moving slowly across to the table to pick up a cookie, he glanced down the hallway. A rug was pushed up against the door of a storage closet.

It didn't look right.

Ambling to the wall, he kept his back to Patty and Jeb as he pretended to admire a collection of cameo paintings, but he was studying the short, narrow passageway.

He caught sight of a plug in a powerpoint.

The wire disappeared under the rug, but he couldn't see where it led.

Turning away, he strolled back to the table and stood behind Jeb.

"When you left Luke Larson, he was very angry, and you didn't see him again that night," Jeb declared.

"That's correct," Patty said emphatically.

"Did you have any further contact with him during the following days?"

"No, thank goodness," Patty replied with a dramatic sigh. "I'm so glad I got away when I did. I could have been the one conked on the head."

"Excuse me," Alex interrupted, "may I use your bathroom?"

"Of course, it's off my bedroom," she said with a smile. "It's the door on the right halfway down the hall. You can't miss it."

"Let's get back to the phone call," Jeb continued as Alex walked away.

Walking slowly down the narrow passageway, Alex kept his eyes on the ground, searching for where the wire emerged. Finally, though it was barely discernible, he spotted it coming out from under the carpet and into the door frame of the closet. Carrying his gaze upward, he discovered it had been covered in white tape, then tied around the handle.

A chill pricked his skin.

Patty Jamison was prepared to electrocute anyone who dared to peek behind the door.

Unnerved by the startling discovery, he took a breath, then moved into the bedroom. Though there appeared to be nothing out of place, something wasn't right—something he couldn't put his finger on. Entering the compact bathroom, he waited a moment, flushed the toilet and washed his hands, then opened the medicine cabinet.

Makeup.

No prescriptions, not even aspirin.

It was odd.

Most people kept a variety of over-the-counter remedies for minor ailments.

Returning to the dining room, he found Jeb on his feet thanking the young woman for her time.

"If anything should pop into your mind, perhaps a comment he made that you might have forgotten, anything at all, please call me."

"I will, and I hope you catch him soon. I'm a bit nervous with him on the loose."

"We believe he's left town, but we're keeping our eyes and ears open," Jeb assured her as they moved to the front door. "Thanks for the coffee."

"Goodbye, Patty," Alex said, amazed the pleasant young woman was capable of boobytrapping her hall closet.

"Nice to have met you. Stay safe out there."

As they walked back to the car, Patty stood on the porch smiling and waving.

"I'm not sure about her," Jeb muttered as they neared the car.

"You've got that right," Alex declared, then waiting until she had closed the door and they were in the car, he added, "She's got a closet door wired to electrocute anyone who tries to open it."

"Say, what?" Jeb exclaimed. "Are you serious?"

"Yep. That's extreme. What could be so important?"

"Drugs? Guns? Hell, it could be almost anything," Jeb replied as he headed back to the main road. "Jewelry, her life savings, who knows?"

"I've gotta hunch it isn't any of those things," Alex said quietly, "and I don't know why, but her bedroom—there's something off—I just can't put my finger on what it is."

"We'll need more than one of your hunches to get a search warrant."

"I've got a feelin' about that as well," Alex said confidently. "We just need to be patient."

AS THE TRAIN CHUGGED into the Longville station, Luke slowly opened his eyes. He had spent the entire trip thinking about Tess. He'd pictured her beautiful breasts, the way she moaned when he kissed her neck, her yelps when he spanked her, and the way she had eagerly surrendered.

His future was with her.

A future he wanted badly.

In the days before his arrest, he'd ached to take her to bed and introduce her to his dark, decadent ways, but in spite of the sparks crackling between them, he had taken things slowly. Now the dire circumstances had thrown their relationship into warp speed. Staring out the window and watching Longville come into view, his brow creased with worry.

In spite of the danger, it was obvious Tess was enjoying the drama. Once things settled down, would she still be as excited, still so full of fire, still thrill to his dominant touch?

The train slowed, then stopped. Staying in the character of an elderly hobo, he slowly rose to his feet, then pretended to struggle as he slipped on the tattered jacket.

"Can I help you," a young woman asked.

"That's real nice of you," Luke replied, making his voice sound husky. "I can manage. It's just the lining. It's ripped from the sleeve."

"You should stop by the church. It's on Third Street. The pastor there has a supply of used clothing. I'm sure he'll be able to find you something better."

"Thank you, I'll do that," Luke said, amazed by her kindness.

Giving him a sympathetic smile, she moved past him and left the train.

Waiting until all the passengers had disembarked, and remembering to stoop as he walked, he headed to the bus stop outside the station.

It was a cool but sunny day. Ideal weather to take Tess on a long ride to the back of his property with a blanket and a bottle of wine. Telling himself their time would come, he decided to sit in the park and watch the ducks.

"Do any of these buses go to Parnell Park?" he asked a teenage boy lounging against the back of one of the shelters.

"Yeah. Number 24. It'll be along in a minute."

Thanking him, Luke sat down to wait. Thinking about the phone in his pocket, he realized it would be unwise to leave it in a bus or taxi. If it was found, there was a possibility Tess, Dwayne, and Robbie's numbers could be retrieved, even if he deleted them. That would cause trouble for them all. Pulling it from his pocket, he sent the first five photographs to Jeb and Alex's phones, then to Jeb's email. As he finished, the bus rolled to a stop in front of him. Climbing on board, he settled in to watch from the window as the town gilded past him.

When it stopped at the park, he stepped off and wandered into the beauty of the trees, flower beds and expansive lawns. Finding an empty bench at the lake's edge, he retrieved his phone and sent the remaining seven pictures, but this time adding a note.

Yes, it's me, Luke Larson. These are posted in Patty Jamison's hall closet, but the door is wired to electrocute anyone who attempts to open it. The plug is in a point half way down the hall. The wire runs beneath the carpet.

For the record, I have never attempted to force myself on any woman, and regardless of the evidence, I did not hurt old Nate, nor did I rob him. I believe Patty Jamison was solely responsible, and she stole the crowbar from my truck and used it to incriminate me.

Her motive? We had been seeing each other for a short time. When I told her it was over, she didn't take it well.

If you enter her cabin and she's not at home, be extremely careful. She has set up trip wires above the threshold of the back door, and nail boards beneath the window.

She once told me she has a collection of shoe boxes containing her secret papers—whatever that means. I don't know where they're kept. They used to be in the closet. If you execute a search warrant, they might be worth finding.

I will not be returning until I receive word you have arrested someone else for the crime for which I was wrongly convicted.

LL

He read it through, then stared at the calm waters of the small lake with its modest fountain. Sighing deeply as he hit the send button, he watched the animated envelope fly through the air and into the mailbox.

"What I wouldn't give to see the looks on their faces," he muttered.

Rising to his feet, he wandered across to the nearest trash bin, opened the phone and dropped in the battery. Leaving the park, he meandered down the main street, depositing various parts of the phone down several different drains, then ambled into a coffee shop.

Buying a large mug of coffee, he sat at an outside table and pulled out the plastic tub so carefully packed by Tess. He was devouring a sandwich when he spotted several patrol cars rolling slowly down the street.

He grinned.

The location of the cell towers had been determined, the alarm had been raised, and he had no doubt Jeb Parker and several of his deputies would soon be arriving in Longville.

CHAPTER NINETEEN

DWAYNE HAD BEEN CALLED back to work. Reluctantly reporting for duty, he was sitting at his desk filling out a report when he saw Jeb dash from his office. Watching him race past, Dwayne suddenly spotted Alex marching towards Jeb from the opposite direction. As the two men met up and began talking excitedly, Dwayne grinned.

Luke had sent the pictures.

In a matter of moments the deputies were summoned into the conference room. Lumbering in, Dwayne found Jeb and Alex powering up the large screen computer. The deputies crowded around, then his uncle, the Sheriff himself, strode through the door.

"Luke Larson just sent a collection of photographs to Alex and me," Jeb announced. "He claims they were in a locked, boobytrapped closet at Patty Jamison's cabin. It fits with what we learned when we were there this morning."

The bizarre assortment of images began appearing on the screen, ending with the large blow up showing Luke's eyes scratched out and a dagger through his heart.

"As you can see, this woman is obsessed with the man. We must consider her unstable, possibly dangerous," Jeb continued. "We're still tryin' to fit the pieces together, but she's now a person of interest for the robbery and attack on Nate. Yep, it's lookin' like Luke Larson is innocent after all."

As a murmur rippled through the gathering, a deep frown carved Dwayne's forehead. At the breakfast table, he'd seen the photographs on Tess's laptop. Viewing them on a large screen he was noticing details. Moving to the side of the huddled group to get a better look, he stared at an unidentifiable object jutting out from behind a newspaper clipping of Luke's arrest. "Hey, Jeb, I think I see—" Dwayne began.

"What?" the sheriff barked, interrupting him. "Speak up boy." Intimidated by his uncle, and knowing the men mocked him behind his back, Dwayne rarely offered input about anything, but Tess and Luke had given him a newfound confidence. Squaring his shoulders, he raised his head and faced the group.

"I see something that might be evidence."

"What? Where?" Jeb demanded. "Show us."

Pushing his way past the deputies standing in front of him, Dwayne pointed to the corner of the screen.

"Isn't that the thumb of a glove?"

Leaning in and staring at the odd shape peeking out from behind the clipping, he hovered the cursor over the area and zoomed in.

"Dwayne, you're right," he exclaimed. "That's exactly what it is, but why is it there?"

"Maybe it's one of the gloves she used when she attacked old Nate and robbed him," Dwayne suggested, "and she put it behind those articles about Luke's arrest, sort of like she's braggin'."

"A twisted mind like that," Alex muttered, glancing up at Dwayne, "yeah, could be. Sheriff, is there enough here to get a search warrant?"

"I'll make sure of it," the Sheriff boomed. "Dwayne, good job, good job."

As his uncle marched from the room, Dwayne broke into a rare smile.

"Okay, fellas, let's get a tail on her, see where she goes and who she hangs out with," Jeb declared, "but make sure you keep your distance."

"She goes to Barry's Bar," Dwayne offered. "We could talk to the people who work there."

"That's right, I saw her there last night," Jeb remarked. "Thanks for remindin' me. Alex, head on over there, see what you can find out."

"Excuse me, Jeb," a voice called from the door. "The cell phone that sent the photographs. I've pinned it down. The signal came from the shopping area in Longville. It's dead now though. It's either been turned off or dumped."

"Longville?" Jeb repeated. "Dammit! I guess I'm goin' back there."

Directing several of the deputies to join him on his manhunt, and selecting a team to start the surveillance, he excused the rest of the men. "Hey, Jeb," Alex said quietly, moving closer to him. "Remember when we left this mornin' and I said I had the feelin' there was something off about her place? I know what it was. There were no pictures anywhere. No vacation snaps, no photos with a boyfriend, no relatives, nothin'. Do you know anyone who has zero personal pictures in their house?"

"Damn," Jeb muttered.

"No photo's anywhere...except in that closet." "That's totally weird," Dwayne muttered, still in the room and staring at the images on the computer.

"About as weird as it gets," Jeb remarked. "After you've finished at Barry's Bar, dig into her past. I'm off to Longview." "What do you want me to do, Jeb?" Dwayne asked. "With Larson in Longville and Tess workin', you can probably move back to your place—as long as Tess feels okay about it, but keep drivin' by her house and Luke's ranch. The sheriff was right. Good job, Dwayne."

"Thanks, Jeb," he said with a grin, and walking away to the locker room to change into his uniform, he chuckled happily.

WITH DWAYNE AT WORK and Luke in Longville, Tess was alone for the first time since Luke had walked into her cafe. The house felt empty, and she was grateful Rex was padding around at her side.

"Sorry, big guy," she murmured as she petted his head. "I have to go to work in a little while, but your daddy will stop by and check on you soon."

The big dog let out a whine and raised his paw.

"You are so cute," she said softly, leaning over and giving him a hug. "When Luke gets back I'm going to suggest we get a dog just like you."

Her butterflies suddenly fluttered. "I need you, Luke," she whispered. "I need you with me. I hope things won't change when you're cleared. I hope this incredible feeling isn't because of all the craziness around us."

Sighing heavily and climbing on the bed, she laid on her back and closed her eyes, lightly tweaking a nipple just like he did when he made love to her. Moving her other hand between her legs, she smiled as she touched her pussy naked beneath her skirt. Before he'd left, he'd forbidden her to wear panties. She'd felt scandalous as she'd driven him to the train station.

"It's something for me to think about while I'm gone," he'd whispered. Rubbing urgently, she recalled his breath in her ear, and the tantalizing feelings that surged through her when she was across his lap and about to be spanked. A combination of nervous anticipation, and a deep, aching carnal need. Increasing the pressure as she continued to massage her clit, she saw visions of him walking towards her carrying *that look* in his eye. An unexpected rush flowed through her body.

Surrendering to the delicious tingling as it moved through her limbs, she sighed heavily. The warm, rippling orgasm had been pleasant, but nothing like the thrilling climaxes he offered.

But she couldn't lie on her bed and ponder.

It was time to change her clothes and return to the cafe. Hoping Jeb had received the photographs and would investigate Patty Jamison, and Luke was safe in his disguise, she dressed quickly and headed back to the living room.

"I wish I could take you with me," she said, giving Rex another hug. "I'll turn the television on. That will keep you company."

But as she picked up the remote control, her landline rang.

She frowned.

Everyone contacted her on her cellphone.

Thinking it would be a random telemarketer, she picked up the receiver. "Hey, Tess, it's me, Patty Jamison. I'm so glad you're listed. We forgot to exchange phone numbers."

As a wave of panic sent a chill down her spine, she closed her eyes and told herself to remain calm.

"Hi, Patty. It's good to hear from you," she managed, "but I'm just running out the door. I need to get to the cafe."

"How about I swing by for dinner? I have a feeling you're a terrific cook. We could share Luke Larson stories."

Tess paused.

If Patty was at the restaurant after the early evening rush, they'd be able to talk, and there'd be no danger chatting at the cafe.

"The best time to come would be around eight, otherwise I'll be too busy to talk."

"Great, I'll bring my appetite." "Super. I'll see you there."

Hanging up the phone, Tess kissed Rex on the head.

"This is fantastic," she said with a grin. "I won't be alone with the crazy lady, but I'll be able to have a natter with her. I have a feeling it's going to be a very good night. You guard the house. Dwayne will be by to check on you."

The large dog looked at her with a soulful expression. Staring into his big brown eyes, Tess knew if anyone approached the house, he'd bark, but if he could, he'd open the door and lead the way to the family silver.

"You're adorable," she muttered, and turning on the television, she grabbed her coat and headed into the garage.

DRIVING INTO THE PARKING lot at Barry's Bar, Alex noticed only a few cars. He wasn't surprised. Though the tavern opened at midday and offered lunch, it was known as an evening hangout. Able to park directly in front of the entrance, he walked inside and up to the counter.

"Can I help you?"

The man behind the bar was stocky and middle-aged. Alex suspected he was the owner.

"I understand you have a regular customer by the name of Patty Jamison."

"Sure do, but I don't know her very well. You need to speak with my bartender, Daniel Griswald. He works most nights."

"Is he around?"

"Yep, just arrived. Hold on a sec."

The man strode to the swinging doors and poked his head through.

"Hey, Daniel, someone wants to speak to you," he called, then ambled back to Alex. "The name's Barry Hardcastle. I own this place. Is there a problem, deputy?"

"I'm just looking for some background information," Alex replied vaguely.

"Hey, are you looking for me?"

Looking across to the doors, Alex saw a tall, wide-shouldered, handsome young man walking towards him.

"Not you specifically," Alex replied.

The bartender was good-looking, clean cut, and well dressed. Alex also noticed the expensive watch around his wrist, and the belt around his waist appeared to be alligator. Not cheap, and not affordable on a barkeeps salary.

"Let's sit down at a quiet table," Alex said, wishing he wasn't in uniform. "Quiet as in private?" Daniel quipped with a grin.

"Exactly," Alex replied, grinning back, "and bring a beer. Whatever's on tap."

"Really? You can drink on duty?"

"Nope, but I need to relax a bit. I hate askin' personal questions, and havin' a beer in my hand seems to help. The name's Alex, by the way. I don't stand with formality."

Alex had learned people responded better to a friendly conversation, and being upfront put subtle pressure on them to do the same. But as Alex studied Daniel's face, he spotted a wariness that usually suggested a checkered past.

"Dealt much with the law?" he asked casually.

"Let's just say, I've learned the law, as you put it, tends to only see what it wants to see," Daniel said, pouring the beer, "and rushes to conclusions, often mistaken conclusions."

Pulling out his wallet, Alex dropped a five dollar bill on the counter.

"That should cover the beer and five minutes of your time."

As Daniel rang up the sale and dropped the change in the tip jar, Alex carried his drink to a corner table and sat down. Calling his boss to cover the counter, Daniel took his time ambling across the room.

"So, what can I help you with," he asked, pulling out a chair.

"First, tell me about this issue you have—or should I say had—with the justice system. Off the record. Think of me as just another guy sittin' at your bar."

"Maybe another time." "Okay," Alex said, deciding not to push. "What can you tell me about Patty Jamison?"

Alex hadn't anticipated Daniel's response.

He crossed his arms.

An odd look flickered in his eyes.

His jaw tightened.

An angry frown lined his forehead.

The body language signified anger. And it ran deep.

"Can I ask why?"

"She's a person of interest in a case we're investigating. Has she seemed edgy lately? Is there anything out of the ordinary you've noticed? I'd like to hear whatever you have to tell me."

"I would say," Daniel began slowly, "Patty Jamison is a woman worth your time. I would suggest you learn more about her past. Now if you'll excuse me, I need to get back to work."

"That's it?"

"I'm sure you have access to an endless variety of data bases," Daniel replied, rising to his feet. "Push the buttons and click."

Alex hadn't touched his beer, and watching the young man stride back to the bar, he picked up the glass and took a drink.

"I sure would like to know your story," he muttered. "I've gotta feelin' you and Patty Jamison have a connection."

CHAPTER TWENTY

SITTING IN THE WAITING room of the Longville train station, Luke watched the local deputies nail up a new Luke Larson wanted poster. A mischievous miscreant had vandalized the previous one, adding thick glasses around Luke's eyes and a goatee on his chin.

"Get yourself some decent grub," one of the deputies said, handing Luke a five dollar bill as he left.

Peering up at him through the darkly tinted, round specs, Luke suppressed a chuckle.

"Much obliged," he mumbled, thinking he'd return it when he was cleared, along with a six pack.

Boarding was called, and keeping up the pretense, Luke limped slowly to the platform and into the train. As he settled into the seat, his thoughts turned to Tess. A smile crossed his lips. At his first opportunity he'd introduce her to bondage, and spank her for pleasure, not punishment. The thought sent his cock to life, and though he attempted to subdue the hunger in his tattered trousers, the image of her naked body and her bright red backside refused to leave his head.

Waiting impatiently until the train had departed and picked up speed, he headed to the men's room. Dressed as he was, he felt almost at odds as he unzipped the old fly and withdrew his sergeant at arms standing at full attention. Leaning against the wall, he closed his eyes and saw his beautiful Tess with her legs spread wide, but she wasn't on the bed, she was outside on a blanket, and her wrists were tied together above her head.

Fervently stroking his cock, he imagined her writhing against his teasing fingers, then a moment later, bent over a downed tree trunk, the blanket between her skin and the rough wood. He was seated beside her, spanking her lustily, then his fingers slid between her cheeks. She squirmed her protest, but he was having none of it, and grabbing a small stick, he flicked it against her reddened behind.

His cock suddenly jerked in his hand, spouting its cream across his hand. "Oh, Tess," he groaned as the spasms waned, "just wait until I get home."

THE EARLY EVENING RUSH had ended early, but the usual wave of latecomers hadn't appeared. Tess put it down to a late breaking weather bulletin warning of a bad storm gathering force and about to descend on the town. She'd sent her two waitresses home, and was about to call Patty to tell her she was closing when the door opened and Patty waltzed in wearing a wide grin. Tess's heart skipped. Unless some customers arrived she'd be alone with the crazy woman after all.

"Hi, Tess. Wow. Where is everybody?"

"I was about to call you. I'm closing up. A storm is about to kick up and I want to beat it home."

"I didn't hear about any storm, but I did notice it was getting windy. Shoot. Could I grab a cup of coffee before I go?"

"Sure," Tess replied. "Have a seat and I'll bring it over."

"Actually, could you point me to the ladies room?"

"It's the door against the far wall," Tess replied, pointing across the room.

"Thanks."

Patty ambled away, and as Tess poured the hot brew, she noticed a flash of headlights swinging into the parking lot. Letting out a breath of relief, she carried the mug to a table by the window, but glancing outside she couldn't see the car.

"So guess what?" Patty declared, snatching her attention. "I had a visit from your brother this afternoon. He said they're looking into Nate's robbery again, though I can't imagine why."

"Huh. Were you able to help him?"

"Not at all, but I have to tell you what happened with the cute bartender last night."

DWAYNE HAD PULLED INTO the parking lot, rolled to a stop and turned off his lights, but as he was about to leave his car and enter the cafe, he spotted Patty Jamison join Tess at a table by the window.

"This isn't good," he muttered. "Luke won't like this one bit."

Not sure what to do, he reached for the phone Luke had given him and called Robbie.

"Hi, Dwayne. How are you? Crazy night, huh?"

"Robbie, I've gotta problem," he said hastily. "Patty and Tess are alone inside the cafe."

"Why don't you go in and join them?"

"Have you spoken to Luke? Did he tell you about Tess and me meetin' her at Barry's Bar?"

"Yep. He called me from the train station before he left for Longville and brought me up to speed, then sent me those insane pictures."

"The thing is," Dwayne continued, "I'm in uniform, and I'm not sure what Patty will think if she sees I'm a deputy."

"Ah, now I understand. You're right! You just never know with a nut job like that. Can she see your car?"

"I'm not sure. She hasn't looked down here. It's dark and the rain's startin'."

"Stay there and keep watch. Even if she sees the patrol car, she won't know it's you. Luke's train arrives in about thirty-minutes and I'm gonna be there. He shouldn't be goin' through those woods in a storm. I'll make sure he knows and we'll come right over."

"Okay, thanks Robbie."

Ending the call, Dwayne noticed Tess leave the table. Patty turned her head and looked out the window. He caught his breath. Remembering Alex would be at the Sheriff's office, he decided to let him know what was happening.

"I don't like the sound of this," Alex said solemnly. "There's a very important errand I have to run, but I'll swing by there as soon as I'm done."

"That would be really good," Dwayne said gratefully. "I don't feel right, if you know what I mean."

"Sure, Dwayne. I know what you mean. Hang tight."

ALEX HAD BEEN RESEARCHING Daniel Griswald and had just hit pay dirt. Ending the call with Dwayne, he grabbed his coat and headed out the door. The old case file had told Alex who Daniel was, and why he'd come to town, and Alex had to make sure the handsome bartender didn't do anything stupid.

Walking outside and met by freezing rain, he grimaced as he thought about the drive to Barry's Bar, but he had no choice. He'd tried to call but couldn't get through, and assumed the storm had knocked out the telephone line.

Turning into the slick street, he drove slowly forward. Though the popular nightspot wasn't far, the drive seemed to take forever, but he finally spotted the glow of Barry's bright pink neon sign. There were only a few cars out front, and parking as close to the entrance as he could, he made a mad dash through the torrential rain and burst inside. The smattering of customers glanced up, then returned to their drinks and conversation. Barry was standing behind the counter.

"Sure is a bad night," Barry declared as Alex approached.

"I'm looking for Daniel," Alex said quickly, not interested in talking about the weather.

"You just missed him. He said he had something urgent to take care of so I let him go. It's not exactly hopping in here."

"Did he say where he was going?"

"Nope, just said it couldn't wait and took off."

"Thanks, and by the way, your landline is dead."

"Yeah, I know. I'll be closing shortly."

But Alex barely heard him.

He was worried Daniel would get himself electrocuted...or maybe worse.

DRIVING SLOWLY THROUGH the downpour to the train station, Robbie wasn't worried about his bright red truck being conspicuous. It was dark, the streets were virtually empty, and the heavy pickup was a safer bet in bad weather than Luke's old Cadillac. Turning into the parking area, he fought the wind as he climbed from the truck, and hurried into the waiting room. Glancing at the ticket counter, he spied the elderly man watching television in the tiny room behind the glass. The old stations that serviced the small towns on the line, always made Robbie feel as if he'd been transported back in time. Sitting on a bench and leaning against the wall, he decided to check in with Dwayne while he was waiting.

"Hi, Robbie," Dwayne said, sounding slightly out of breath.

"Hey, Dwayne. Anything to report?"

"They're still sittin' there. Tess left for a minute and came back with a basket of fries. Made me hungry. Now they're sharin' a bottle of wine. I'm freezin'. I wish I could turn the engine on and get the heater runnin'. Better yet, I wish I could go inside. I don't understand why Tess hasn't closed up and left. Maybe Patty's talkin'."

"Hang in there, Dwayne. Luke and I will be there soon—in fact—I hear him arrivin' right now."

"Hurry—but drive safely."

"I will, Dwayne. Gotta go."

Ending the call and striding quickly out to the platform, Robbie jogged up to Luke as he stepped off the train.

"I'm really glad to see you," Luke said gratefully.

"There was no way I was gonna let you try to get through the woods in this weather," Robbie declared, pretending to help the old man.

"It's wild how these storms flare up," Luke remarked, "and I can't believe I forgot to take a second phone with me."

"Best laid plans," Robbie muttered.

Moving back through the waiting room and outside to his truck, once inside the warm cab, Luke pulled off the scruffy hat and let out a heavy sigh.

"So, Robbie, any news?"

"I'm afraid so," Robbie replied, leaving the station and turning into the main street.

"That doesn't sound good. Is Tess okay?"

"She's sharin' a bottle of wine with Patty Jamison at the cafe as we speak. Dwayne's parked in front keepin' watch, but he's in uniform so he's worried about goin' in. I promised we'd get there right away."

"Ah, right. He's so much smarter than people give him credit for. Dressed like I am I doubt Patty will recognize me, and if she does I don't care. I have to get Tess outta there."

"Maybe I should go in," Robbie suggested. "If Patty does see through that disguise, she might call the cops. Are you ready for that?"

"Dammit, you're right. Okay, thanks, Robbie. Tell Tess the roads are bad and you're there to take her home. That should work. Is there anything else?"

"Yep. Jeb and several of his deputies went lookin' for you in Longville just like you thought they would, but accordin' to Dwayne, those photographs blew them away. They're interested in Patty now. Like—really interested."

TESS WAS GROWING NERVOUS.

Patty wouldn't leave.

She'd said she was starving.

Tess whipped her up some fries.

Then she'd pulled a bottle of screw cap wine from her bag and insisted Tess join her in a drink.

"It's been ages since I've done this girl-talk thing," Patty remarked.

"Yeah, it's been fun," Tess said, then faked a yawn. "I am getting tired though."

"Have some more wine."

"No thanks, we both have to drive, and it's going to be difficult enough in that awful weather."

"That cop sure has been sitting out there a long time," Patty murmured, leaning across the table. "I wonder why he doesn't come in."

"Cop?" Tess repeated, staring out the window. "I saw headlights earlier, but I figured it was someone using the parking lot to turn around. I still don't see a car."

"He's out there, all right!" Patty exclaimed. "You wouldn't know why, would you? The Deputy Sheriff is your brother."

"I have no idea."

"The thing is, Tess, I met you last night, then this afternoon Jeb and some other dude came out to my cabin, and now there's a deputy parked outside your restaurant. What would you think if you were me?"

Before Tess could answer, powerful headlights shone through the window and illuminated the squad car.

"Holy crap, you're right, there is a patrol car out there," she exclaimed, then recognizing Robbie's truck and knowing Luke would be in the cab, she wanted to jump for joy. "Looks like I have a late night customer. I'll be right back."

"Sure, take your time," Patty answered, pointedly adding, "I'm not going anywhere."

Moving behind the counter, Tess waited expectantly as Robbie pushed through the door.

"Hello," she said happily. "What are you doing out in this storm?"

"I'm so glad you're still here! I just picked up my elderly uncle from the train station and he's tired and hungry. I don't have much at home, so I thought I'd take a chance and see if you were still open."

"You just caught me. What would you like?"

"Do you have any of that tomato vegetable soup left?"

"I sure do. It'll only take a few minutes to heat up. Anything else?"

"A double order of your french fries. They're so good."

"Coming right up. Have a cup of coffee while you're waiting," she offered, pouring him a cup, then headed quickly into the kitchen.

"Hi, Robbie, remember me?"

Robbie slowly turned around.

"Patty Jamison!" he declared, pretending to be surprised. "Sure I remember. You accused my boss of—"

"Hey, I just told the police what happened," she snapped, picking up her bag and marching towards him. "Real odd that you should appear out of nowhere on a night like this. So many coincidences. The thing is, I don't believe in coincidences. All this shit has set off alarm bells in my head."

Tess had placed the fries in the oil, and was about to put the soup in the microwave, but hearing the conversation, she hurried back to the swinging doors and peered through the small round window.

"All what shit?" Robbie demanded. "I don't know what you're talkin' about."

"The thing is, country boy," Patty muttered, walking behind the counter, "I've survived as long as I have because I'm not an idiot," she continued, fishing in her bag. "Do me a favor. Go to the window and wave in that cop. He's been sitting in that car since I got here."

"Why would I do that?"

"Because if you don't," she suddenly growled, pulling out what looked like a large water pistol, "you'll be jerking like a fish on the end of a line. This is a taser. You can either get that cop in here, or he'll burst through the door after he sees you go down. Your choice."

Her heart racing, Tess watched Robbie head to the window and start waving at Dwayne, but she knew he wouldn't be able to see Patty from the parking lot. He'd have no idea the woman was holding a weapon.

"See what happens when you don't do as you're told?"

Spinning around, she found Luke, absolutely drenched and shaking his head.

CHAPTER TWENTY-ONE

STANDING UNDER MINIMAL cover on the porch of Patty's cabin, Alex's heart thumped like a jackhammer. Her car was not in the carport, but a black Range Rover was parked off to the side, and Alex suspected it belonged to Daniel Griswald.

"I wish I'd been drivin' that," Alex muttered under his breath.

His patrol car didn't have four wheel drive, and it had been a treacherous trip up the winding mountain road.

Moving closer to the front door, he strained to listen for any sounds, but the driving wind and pounding rain was all he could hear. Worried about a booby trap, he stood back as he gingerly tried the door handle. To his shock, it turned. Pushing the door open with the toe of his boot, he peered into the cabin and spotted the glow of a moving flashlight.

"Daniel, it's Alex," he called, moving inside and kicking the door shut behind him. "I'm not here to arrest you, I don't care that you broke in."

The flashlight paused.

"You've obviously figured out who I am, so you know why I'm here," Daniel called back. "I couldn't wait. If she finds out you're sniffing around she'll do a bunk and I'll lose her. You people did nothing, so now it's down to me. I have to search this place while I have the chance."

"Don't touch anything," Alex yelled urgently. "She has booby traps all over the place. For God's sake, don't touch anything—and be careful where you walk!"

Pulling his flashlight from his belt and moving the powerful beam around the room, he noticed the pictures he'd pretended to admire earlier in the day were gone, and so were many of her knickknacks. He wondered if Patty Jamison was already packing up to leave. "Daniel, I swear I'm only here to save your ass," Alex continued. "This house is a dangerous place. We both need to leave." As the glow from the hall swung around, Daniel emerged from the passage.

"Save my ass?" he demanded angrily. "Like you guys saved my brother's ass?"

Lightening suddenly illuminated the space.

Alex's uncanny instinct sent his eyes upward.

In the split second, he'd spied a fisherman's net laced with barbed wire above his head.

"Yeah," Alex grunted, shining his flashlight to the ceiling. "Like I said, save your ass."

"What the hell?" Daniel muttered, staring in shock. "How the fuck did she manage that?"

"Daniel, don't move. There'll be a trip wire. I'm amazed one of us hasn't already triggered it."

"Shit—Alex—it's right there—by your feet!"

Shining his light to the floor, Alex saw two wires wrapped around the legs of the coffee table. The closest was stretched across his path inches away. One more step and the hazardous net would have engulfed him. The other wire ran across the width of the living room, ready to trip up anyone who walked through.

"What is it they say?" Alex muttered. "Life is a matter of inches."

"Something like that," Daniel replied, his voice tremulous. "I thought my heart was racing before, now it's about to jump out of my fucking chest." "How did you get in and not fall over these wires?" "I didn't even try the doors, I just figured they'd be locked," Daniel replied. "I climbed in through the bathroom window."

"Damn. She left them open on purpose. She is one evil woman. I assume you haven't found anything."

"I literally just got here. I thought she'd be at home on a night like this. When I found the place empty I decided to do a search."

"Dammit, I have to warn Tess," Alex mumbled, "but let's get out of here first."

"Hey. there's a light switch on this wall," Daniel announced, reaching his hand out.

"No! Don't!" Alex warned sharply. "This crazy bitch knew enough about electricity to wire up a door. Just watch where you put your feet and come on out."

As Daniel shone his flashlight in front of him and moved cautiously over the trip wires, Alex backed up, meeting him at the door.

"This place has creeped me out," Daniel muttered.

"You and me both," Alex replied, "but before we go outside, will you follow me down the hill in case I hit trouble? I have to take my car. I need the radio."

"Can't you just use your cell phone? It's going to be worse now. You should ride with me."

"You might be right," Alex said thoughtfully. "Okay, let's go together in your car. You can tell me how you found Patty Jamison, and exactly what happened with your brother."

Stepping out into the storm, they trudged as quickly as they could through the mud and pouring rain, but were completely soaked by the time they climbed inside Daniel's SUV.

"I have to make that call," Alex declared, peeling off his wet jacket and tossing it in the back seat. "I need to make sure Tess is okay."

Grateful to be in the safety of the heavy, four-wheel drive, he pulled out his cell phone and called Dwayne.

STILL PARKED OUTSIDE the cafe, Dwayne had seen Tess leave the table, then Patty had followed, but now there was no sign of either of them, and Robbie was gesturing for him to come inside.

"This is weird," Dwayne muttered to himself. "He was the one who said it could spook Patty if I went in."

Unsure what to do, he did nothing, then Robbie suddenly threw his hands in the air and disappeared from view.

"That's weird too," Dwayne murmured. "Maybe I should check in with Alex and let him know what's goin' on."

But as he reached for his phone, Sweet Home Alabama rang through the car. Quickly grabbing it and looking at the screen, he couldn't believe it was the man himself.

"Alex, I was just gonna call you!"

"Are you still at the cafe?" Alex asked urgently. "Yep, but I can't see Patty or Tess anymore," Dwayne quickly replied, "and the foreman from Luke's ranch drove up and went inside about fifteen minutes ago. He was at the window wavin' at me, but now he's gone too."

"There's a back way outta there, right?"

"Through a storeroom. Do you think that's why Robbie wanted me to go in, because Patty has taken off?" "Possibly, but I'm more concerned she's still there, and that ranch hand was trying to get your attention to help him."

"Shit. Should I do that, or wait for you?"

"I'm on my way, but it's slow goin' in this weather. Do you think you can arrest Patty for suspicion of GBH and robbery? Don't feel you have to say yes. You have no back up, so I understand if—"

"Hey, Alex, don't worry, I'll be fine," Dwayne assured him, though his heart was beginning to pump. Then wanting to sound like one of the senior deputies, he added, "I'll call you when the situation is contained." "Be careful and be smart. I'll see if there's anyone else in the vicinity, but on a night like this, I expect everyone will be busy handlin' emergencies and accidents."

"If help arrives, great, if it doesn't, I'll deal with what happens," Dwayne said vehemently, determined to apprehend the vile woman who had caused such havoc. "I'm goin' in and I'll get her."

Before Alex could answer, Dwayne ended the call, and taking a deep breath, he stepped into the downpour, drew his gun from its holster, and hurried to the door.

LUKE HAD RIPPED OFF his disguise and peeled off the drenched, oversized coat. Though he was still wearing ill-fitting, baggy trousers, he gave Tess a quick, strong hug, then pulled back and grabbed her forearms.

"Thank God, you're okay," he whispered, staring at her intently. "I'm so happy to see you. Are you all right? Any ideas?"

"I'm great, Longville was easy, but about this situation—I'm not sure yet. For the moment, if Patty calls out, don't answer."

"Okay."

The door buzzer made them both jump.

"Someone else is here," Tess breathed, staring up at him with wide eyes.

Moving quickly to the swinging doors, he peeked through the round window. Dwayne was holding his gun out in front of him, Robbie was tied to a chair, and speaking in a low voice, Patty was holding a taser against his genitals, but Luke couldn't hear a word she was saying.

"What's going on?" Tess whispered.

"Look for yourself," Luke murmured, letting out a sigh of dismay as he stepped back.

Gazing through the tiny window, she saw Patty holding the taser against Robbie, and Dwayne placing his gun on the floor.

"Why did I agree to meet her?" she bleated, dropping her head. "I'm such an idiot."

"We all are at times," Luke said softly, "but right now you need to keep it together."

"Hey, Tess, where are you?" Patty suddenly shouted. "The party's out here."

Gripping Luke's hand, Tess didn't respond.

"Tess!" Patty yelled again. "Come on out or your boyfriend here gets his nuts tasered off."

"Luke, what should I do?"

"Listen," he said softly, lifting his finger to his lips. "Be patient, and just listen. An opportunity will present itself. It always does."

DWAYNE HAD NEVER KNOWN such fury or fright, and though he'd been forced to lay his weapon on the floor, he hadn't given up. He just needed an opening. "Hey, Dudley Do Right," Patty spat, "is there a back door to this place?"

"Yeah," Dwayne managed, "it's through a—"

"Shut up and walk," she barked, pointing the taser at him.

"Uh, where to?"

"Where do you think, you big dummy?"

The words stung.

Dwayne bristled.

He'd get the better of her, even if he died trying.

"I'm waiting," she said impatiently, waving the taser at him.

White hot anger seething through him, he headed towards the kitchen, but as he approached the swinging doors an idea flashed through his head. If he was far enough in front, he'd be able to push the door back into Patty's face.

"Let Tess know we're coming in," Patty ordered. "Quickly."

"Tess, I'm walkin' through the doors," Dwayne declared, "and Patty's behind me with the—" but abruptly charged forward before finishing.

Caught off guard, it took a second for Patty to hurry after him, but as she dashed into the kitchen, she suddenly tripped and tumbled to the floor.

"Fuck, fuck, my knee!" she wailed, her body sprawled on the hard tile and the taser spilling from her fingers.

Grabbing Tess's hand, Luke hastily pulled her into the dining room.

Spinning around, shocked to see her on the ground, Dwayne swiftly straddled her waist and cuffed her wrists behind her back. Though feeling triumphant as he stood up, he stared around the empty room bewildered, wondering how the girl had ended up on the kitchen floor.

He hadn't seen Luke flat against the wall, darting his foot in Patty's path as she'd entered.

Leaving her where she was, Dwayne strode into the restaurant and found Luke and Tess untying Robbie. Overjoyed Luke was safe, Dwayne marched forward and threw his arms around him.

"I'm sure glad you're okay. When did you arrive?" "I'm better than okay," Luke replied, awkwardly extricating himself from the big guy's unexpected embrace, "and you were great in there."

"You mean in the kitchen? Hang on," Dwayne muttered, a frown crossing his forehead. "Is that how Patty fell? Were you in there? Did you trip her up?"

"Listen carefully," Luke said gravely, "I was never here. It was Tess who did that."

"But—you're a hero!"

"No arguments. This is your shining moment, not mine."

"But—"

"Dwayne, I'm not ready to be taken in yet, and I don't want Tess or you gettin' in trouble for helpin' me. I was never here. Wait until after Robbie and I leave, then call it in. I'll see you back at Tess's house."

"How do I explain why Robbie took off? Alex knows he was here."

"Say he got himself free while you and Tess were in the kitchen, but he didn't have his cellphone, so he ran to his truck to call for help, then he had to leave because of his elderly uncle. Don't worry, I'll make sure he calls 911. Got it?"

"Yeah, sure," Dwayne replied. "Hey, Robbie, are you all right?"

"Aside from having a heart attack when that crazy bitch had a taser against my willy, I'm fine. What about you?"

"I'm really happy we caught Patty Jamison and everyone's okay."

"What about you, Tess?" Robbie asked, as she finished untying his ankles. "You haven't said a word."

"I'm really sorry, Robbie. I should never have agreed to meet that cow. I feel terrible about all this." "We don't have time to discuss that now," Luke declared. "Robbie and I have to get out of here, oh, and get rid of the fake hair, the coat, all the stuff I took off before Alex gets here."

"No problem, and I'll see you soon," she murmured. "Please be careful."

"I won't be a wanted man much longer," he said softly, and giving her a quick hug, he and Robbie hurried to the door. "Hey, Tess, I'll be right back. I wanna check on our prisoner," Dwayne said as Luke and Robbie disappeared into the parking lot. "Wait, I'm coming with you."

As they entered the kitchen, Patty twisted her head and glared up at them over her shoulder.

"Where the fuck were you? I need a fucking ambulance. My knee is killing me."

"You be quiet," Dwayne growled, using a voice Tess never thought him capable of, "and you'd better stop with that foul language or I'll gag you."

"Bastard."

"Yeah, maybe, but I'm a smart bastard, not some dummy lying handcuffed on a kitchen floor!"

CHAPTER TWENTY-TWO

LEAVING THE CAFE AND heading to Tess's house, Robbie made the 911 call and quickly explained the situation, then apologized for leaving the scene.

"I'm with my elderly uncle and I have to get him home, but you have my phone number if you need to reach me."

As he ended the call, two squad cars, their sirens blaring and lights flashing, drove past him.

"Dwayne must have called it in as soon as we left," Luke declared. "They'll be at the cafe shortly. Too bad Jeb's not with them. I hope he makes it home okay from Longville in this storm."

"It's been a helluva night," Robbie muttered, "and that Patty Jamison is one crazy bitch. I was quakin' in my boots."

"We all were," Luke remarked with a weary sigh. "I wonder how many other men she's victimized."

"I can't wait to get home. First thing I'm gonna do is down a large scotch," Robbie declared. "I don't think I've ever needed a drink like I do right now."

"Speakn' of home, did you have any trouble with the horses?"

"I brought them all in the minute I heard the weather alert," Robbie replied. "Dusty's a real sweet mare. Like her momma though, feisty as all get out."

"Yeah, Tess is that," Luke said with a grin "but I wouldn't change her. Tame her a bit maybe, but not change her."

"Tame? Ha!" Robbie exclaimed, shooting Luke a look. "Good luck with that, but I'll bet you'll have fun tryin.'"

Luke chuckled.

"I'm sure I will."

"Now Patty's been arrested, the sheriff will get to the bottom of this mess and you'll have your life back."

"From your lips to God's ear," Luke said with a sigh. "I sure as hell hope so, but they need hard evidence, and I don't see her as the confessin' type. I'm just hopin' when they search her place they'll find something to nail her ass."

"They're bound to," Robbie said optimistically, turning down the alley that would take them to the back of Tess's home. "Here we are, but you don't have a coat. I could drive around the block and park behind the garage. It'll be a lot closer to the front door. Wouldn't that be easier for you than the back yard? You'll be soaked by the time you get inside."

"I'm not takin' any chances at this stage, and I'll be under a shower in five minutes anyway. Thanks for everything. I don't need to say drive carefully, but I will anyway. Drive carefully and get back to the ranch in one piece." "I will. Lord knows I don't need anymore drama tonight."

Stepping from the truck, Luke pushed open the gate and hurried through the torrent, quickly finding the key in its usual hiding place. Sliding it in the lock, he heard a threatening bark, but pushing open the door, Rex jumped up excitedly, almost knocking him down.

"I'm happy to see you too, fella," he declared, petting him as he kicked the door shut. "Get off me and I'll find you a treat."

The dog barked again, but sat down and stared at Luke expectantly.

Not wanting to trek water through the house, Luke stripped off where he stood, but as the garments hit the floor, Rex sniffed the dirty, wet clothes, and promptly lifted his leg.

"Really?" Luke exclaimed. "Good grief. You probably needed to go out, you poor thing. Hopefully Dwayne will be here soon and he'll take you home." Lifting a wooden spoon from the decorative copper bucket on the counter, he opened the door and pushed the clothes outside.

Tess had left the television on to keep Rex company, and some of the lights burning so the dog wouldn't be left in the dark when the sun went down, but the heat was on low. Naked and shivering, Luke turned up the thermostat, gave Rex a rawhide, then moved quickly down the hallway and into the bathroom. Gratefully standing under a stream of hot water, he soaped away the grime from the day and the cold of the night, then toweled off and crawled into bed. Closing his eyes, he sank into the mattress, utterly and completely exhausted.

THE CAFE BUZZED WITH activity.

Alex and Daniel had arrived, along with four other deputies in two squad cars. Patty had been placed in one of them, Tess and Dwayne had given an account of what happened to Alex, and though it was late, he asked Dwayne to return to the station to write the report.

"It's a good idea to do it while things are fresh in your mind," Alex declared, "and it also means you won't have to come back in the morning."

"Yeah, sure. I want to get it out of the way," Dwayne replied, then walked across to Tess, busy behind the counter pouring mugs of fresh brewed coffee for the deputies.

"Hey, Tess, I have to go back to the station. Can you take care of Rex for me? I don't know how long I'll be, so I'll come by in the mornin.'"

"Of course," she replied, then glanced out the window as she caught sight of Patty being driven away.

"Looks like she won't be causin' any more trouble," Dwayne remarked, following Tess's gaze. "I hope they put her away."

"Dwayne, you've been an absolute superhero," Tess said gratefully. "Thank you for everything."

"Uh, well, uh, you're welcome," he replied, his face blushing red. "I'd better get to the station."

As he strode away, Tess noticed the handsome bartender sitting at a table in the corner of the room. Pouring an extra cup of coffee, she placed it on a tray with milk and sugar, and carried it over to him.

"Hi, Daniel, sorry to meet you again in such difficult circumstances," she said, placing it in front of him. "I thought you could probably use this."

"Great, yeah," he said, adding the cream and a packet of sugar and taking a drink. "Man, that's good."

"Do you mind if I join you?"

"Not at all. I'm sure you have questions."

"I do, like, why did you and Alex show up together? It has to be more than coincidence."

"I was at Patty's searching her house when Alex showed up." "You were searching? That sounds like the middle of the story, not the beginning."

"You're right, sorry. It started with my brother. He got involved with a woman called Jamie Patterson. Long story short, she accused him of rape—"

"Wait," Tess interrupted, "Jamie Patterson? Is that Patty Jamison?"

"Yep, one and the same. Clever huh? Patty Jamison is her real name."

"Unbelievable. Sorry, I didn't mean to interrupt. What happened with your brother?"

"He was arrested and convicted, but Patty had concocted the whole thing. She'd stolen about twenty grand from him, along with some watches and other things. The day after the trial she vanished. I finally tracked her down with the help of a private detective. It wasn't easy. We thought her name was Jamie Patterson. Anyway, I didn't have much of a plan when I arrived here, except winning her trust then searching her house and hoping to find something...anything...that might help his cause."

"She didn't know you?"

"I was in England—Oxford to be precise—when she pulled her shit on my brother. I've focused on nothing but finding her and getting him out of prison since I got back."

"How did Alex connect you to Patty?"

"My investigator had contacts in the police department, and he made sure Jamie Patterson's legal name, Patty Jamison, was in the file. Uncovering her identity wasn't enough to get my brother cleared, but he knew it would return a hit if anyone started digging because of a similar crime, and that's exactly what happened. Alex came looking for me because he was worried about what I might do if I found that conniving bitch." "Thank God he did," Tess exclaimed, "and tell that investigator thank you from me!"

"Hello, Tess," Alex said, approaching the table. "I take it Daniel has filled you in."

"He has. What happens now?"

"We'll be searching Patty's cabin tomorrow. If she incriminated Luke Larson the way Daniel believes she framed his brother, we might find the evidence to clear both of them, though I think it's clear Patty attacked old Nate and pinned it on Luke. We just don't have a motive."

"You don't need one with that lunatic," Daniel grunted. "My brother's only sin was ending their relationship."

"That's what Luke did!" Tess exclaimed. "Alex, that's her motive! Revenge for being dumped!"

"Damn," Alex muttered. "I'm glad you said that, Daniel. Suddenly it all makes sense, but Luke is still a wanted man. He escaped the pen. That's a crime in itself."

"What are you talking about?" Tess demanded, jumping to her feet. "You guys got it wrong. That's not Luke's fault. He had no choice. He had to get out to prove he was innocent. You should be thanking him, not hunting him. In fact, he should sue you and the whole damn department!"

"Hey, easy, girl," Alex said patiently. "We're not perfect, and—"

"I'm not a fucking horse," she yelled. "Don't you dare tell me to take it easy. You ruined a man's life. You and your deputies are no better than the Keystone Cops. Dwayne's the only one who's worth his salt."

"Dwayne? Why would you say that?"

"He cares about what's right, unlike everyone else around here, including my brother. Are you finished? I need to lock up and go home."

"Yeah, we're done," Alex replied, keeping his voice measured. "We've processed the scene and you can open as usual tomorrow. Can I walk you to your car?"

"You? Not a chance. If someone wanted to grab my purse, you'd probably arrest me for carrying the fucking thing." As a frown crossed his face, Tess realized she may have gone too far, but she didn't care. Everything she'd said was true.

"Uh, thanks for the drink," Daniel said, breaking the tension and downing the last of the coffee. "It hit the spot."

"You're welcome," Tess muttered, turning her blazing eyes away from Alex. "Stay safe out there, Daniel," she added, softening her voice. "Please come back for dinner. It's on the house."

"Sounds good. I will. Are you ready, Alex."

"Yep. Goodnight, Tess. Be careful drivin' home."

Crossing her arms, she turned her back on him and walked away, then waited until they'd left before bolting the door.

With the cafe empty, she walked swiftly into the kitchen, grabbed a trash bag, turned out the lights, and moved into the storeroom. Opening the old freezer and retrieving the clothes Luke had discarded, she stuffed them into the plastic bag.

"Thank God I kept this old freezer," she muttered. "I'm never selling it, never."

Heading outside and into the rain, she hurriedly climbed into her car and started the perilous drive home. Finally pulling into her garage, and almost tripping over Rex as she hurried inside, she found the house deathly quiet.

"Luke?" she called, removing her wet coat. "Are you here?"

Receiving no response, and realizing the television had been turned off, she walked quickly down the hallway to her bedroom. Opening the door and looking across the dark room, she saw Luke was in bed, sound asleep.

"You must have been absolutely wiped out, and it's all my fault," she whispered. "You should have been able to come straight home from Longville. Instead you ended up at risk again, rescuing Robbie and me and Dwayne because I didn't listen. I'm so sorry. I'll make it up to you. I don't know how, but I will, I promise."

Deciding to take a shower in the guest bathroom so she wouldn't wake him, she quietly closed the door, but on the way back down the hall, Rex appeared, lifted his paw, then trotted to the front door and whined.

"Of course," she said with a sigh.

Taking some towels from the linen closet in preparation for their return, she donned a long, oilskin coat, stuffed her hair under a hat, and took him for a quick stroll in the front yard.

It felt like forever before she crawled softly into bed, and sighing heavily, she curled up next to the warmth of Luke's muscled body.

He didn't stir.

Closing her eyes, she said a silent thank you, but as she began to fall asleep, Alex's words rang through her head.

Luke is still a wanted man.

She frowned.

"The hell he is asshole," she whispered under her breath. "We'll see about that."

CHAPTER TWENTY-THREE

WAKING LATE THE FOLLOWING morning and finding the bed empty, Tess pulled on her robe and padded down the hallway. She found Luke sitting on the couch in the living room wearing boxers and a T-shirt sporting a very large grin. Rex was nearby, happily chewing on his rawhide.

"Good morning," she said, pecking Luke on the cheek. "You look like you slept well."

"You turned off all the phones," he declared, patting the cushion next to him. "Sit with me."

"Guilty as charged. I wanted us to have a night of undisturbed sleep, and wake up when we felt like it, but why did you mention it?"

"When I got up I decided to check in with Robbie. He's been calling here all mornin'. Apparently those secret boxes Patty was so proud of were stacked in the trunk of her car. It looks like I'm not gonna be a wanted man much longer."

"You're kidding?" she squealed, throwing her arms around his neck. "That's absolutely fantastic."

"Dwayne is on his way here now, supposedly to pick up Rex, but he's really comin' to give us the latest."

"This is the best news ever."

Leaping up and straddling his lap, she began smothering his face with kisses.

"Okay, okay but I'm not one-hundred percent in the clear yet," he said with a chuckle. "I've been AWOL, remember?"

"But what was in the boxes that's going to clear you?" she pressed, ignoring his remark.

"Let me ask you a question. What do you think would be the most incriminatin' thing Patty could've done?"

Luke stared at her happy face as she concentrated on the question, but suddenly spurred by a surge of erotic energy, he brought his hand to the back of her head, clutched her hair, and crushed his lips against hers.

"How can I possibly think about anything when you do that?" she panted as he pulled back.

"I'm glad you can't," he replied with a chuckle, "but give it a shot. The most incriminatin' thing would be...?"

"Um...that would have to be a confession." "You hit the nail on the head," he exclaimed, abruptly jerking the robe from her shoulders. "She had a stack of diaries. The stupid woman wrote detailed accounts of every con she ever pulled, going back to when she was in high-school. She believed her brilliant griftin' career would be a bestsellin' book one day. She called it her retirement."

"Confessions of a Con Artist sounds like a fun read," Tess said with a giggle.

"Secrets of a Sexy Siren would be better," he growled, moving his fingers into her sex. "Oh, girl, you are wet. Get up for a second." As she raised herself onto her knees, he slipped off his boxers and tossed them aside. "Now sit on me," he ordered gruffly, grasping her waist.

Wrapping her fingers around his stiff shaft, she held his cock steady, sank slowly down, then resting her hands on his shoulders for balance, she began the ride. As she found her rhythm, he moved his hands from her waist to clutch her luscious mounds, ravenously devouring her nipples with fervent hunger. Letting out a loud groan, she stayed still and thrust out her chest, relishing the feel of his large member buried deep inside her. But suddenly wrapping his arms tightly around her, he moved them swiftly to the floor, pinned her wrists on either side of her head, and began pummeling her pussy.

"You," he breathed in her ear, "are a very, naughty girl, and you know what happens to naughty girls."

As his scolding threat sent her stomach churning, his concrete cock accelerated.

"You think you're gonna get your bottom warmed," he continued, his wiry chest hairs prickling her nipples, "and you're right, but there's more than just hot ass comin' your way."

Gasping in response to the promised mystery punishment, she threw her legs around his waist.

"You," he announced gruffly as he quickened his pace, "will learn to listen!"

It was all she needed to fly off the cliff.

With a shuddering wail she surrendered to the explosive orgasm.

As the shimmering spasms surged through her body, his cock erupted, joining her euphoric cry with his deep groans. Wave after glorious wave swept them up, until breathless and spent, he collapsed on top of her and sank against her warm, limp body.

"Luke...? she mumbled breathlessly.

"Yeah, baby?"

"You're crushing me."

"Sorry," he muttered, panting heavily as he rolled off her and onto his back.

Still puffing, she rested her head in the crook of his shoulder and snuggled against him.

"I'm so glad Dwayne didn't come knocking," she managed. "I'm not sure we would've heard him, and he knows where the key is."

"Damn, you're right. See what you do to me?"

"Do I muddle your brain?"

"And a whole lot more," he replied, letting out a long, deep breath. "Hey, Tess, I meant what I said."

"I know," she whispered, a flurry of butterflies abruptly fluttering through her belly. "I can't begin to tell you how sorry I am."

"You're willful and stubborn, and I have to admit, there are times when I love that about you, but not when it puts you in harm's way. That's gotta stop."

"I know," she repeated. "I don't understand why I do things sometimes. Things I know I shouldn't, I mean."

"I think it's cos you were a daddy's girl. A big smile and you could do whatever you wanted, right?"

"Maybe...a bit."

"Maybe?"

"Okay, yes, I was," she admitted. "I still am."

"Yep, you are, but that's okay. When I have a little girl, she'll probably have me wrapped around her little finger too."

Raising her eyes, she stared up at the strong, daring, handsome cowboy.

"You'll be an amazing dad," she whispered, heat suddenly flaming in her throat.

Rex, who had been sitting quietly on his pad across the room, unexpectedly jumped up and trotted to the door.

"I guess Dwayne's about to arrive," Tess remarked with a sigh. "I've really enjoyed having that dog here."

"Me too, except for last night, but I'll tell you about that later," Luke said hastily, rising to his feet as he heard footsteps coming up the path. "Luke, get out of here," she said urgently, jumping up as the knock sounded on the door. "We don't know for sure that's Dwayne."

"You're right, I'll stay in the guest room until you call me," he said quietly, grabbing his boxers and hurrying from the room.

Wrapping her robe tightly around her, she padded to the door, shocked to discover Dwayne standing on her porch with Jeb and Alex.

"Uh, hi, why are you all here?"

"We have some good news for Luke," Jeb declared, "and I suspect you know where he is."

"I don't know what you're talking about," she lied. "Dwayne, Rex is ready to go. His leash is—"

"May we come in?" Jeb asked, cutting her off. "It's important, very important."

Glaring at him, she stepped aside, but shot Dwayne a bewildered look as he continued to make a fuss of his dog. "So what's so urgent?" she asked, walking into the living room.

"I need to tell Luke first," Jeb said with a frown. "Don't worry, we're not gonna arrest him."

"Jeb! Just tell me what's going on!"

"Like Jeb said, we need to speak to Luke, but he won't be taken away in handcuffs," Alex said firmly, speaking for the first time. "After everything you did—or should I say—didn't do, you expect me to believe that?"

"Hey, Tess," Jeb said, softening his voice, "Alex is telling the truth, and if anyone has helped him, that's not a problem. They're off the hook. I give you my word as your brother."

"Then I guess it's okay for me to show myself!" Luke declared, entering the room.

Though sporting a five-o'clock shadow, he was dressed in jeans and a clean, white T-shirt, and his hair was combed back off his face.

"I had a feelin' you were here," Alex muttered with a grin. "I'm glad to see you're okay."

"Like you care," Tess grunted.

"Have you been in cahoots with Luke all along?" Jeb suddenly demanded. "Has he been stayin' here?"

"What is this?" she retorted, glaring back at him. "What happened to that speech you just made? *And if anyone has helped him, that's not a problem. They're off the hook*," she scoffed, mimicking his voice. "I think we're digressing," Alex said quickly. "You're right, sorry," Jeb apologized, lowering his voice, "but Tess, this is complicated, so don't interrupt like you usually do."

"I'm not promising anything."

"Of course you're not," Jeb muttered. "That would be too easy."

"Luke, I'll start with the bottom line," Alex began. "In a few hours you'll be free to return home."

"Whoo hoo," Tess shouted. "It's about time! That's awesome."

"Tess, be quiet," Jeb scolded.

"Hey, I'm not going to sit here like some moron and contain myself after hearing news like that."

"The paperwork is bein' prepared," Alex continued, ignoring the bickering siblings, "and I know Dwayne has told you about the diaries. They're still bein' read and analyzed, but I gotta tell you, she brags about how easy it was to steal your crowbar."

"It would've been. It was just sittin' in my toolbox in the garage. I did try to tell you—several times."

"I don't know what to say about that, except we're sorry. If it's any consolation, she wrote some pretty nasty things about the sheriff's department."

"Like what?" Tess interjected. "Tell us. Luke has a right to know."

"Fair enough," Alex replied with a frown. "Like, how stupid we were to fall for such an obvious setup. At one point she almost changed her mind because she thought she'd get caught. Luke, we're all a red-faced right now, and every one of us feels bad about what happened, real bad."

"I'm sorry, Alex, but I can't say it's all right," Luke murmured.

"Because it's not!" Tess exclaimed. "It's not all right at all. None of it is, and don't you dare tell me to shut up, Jeb Turner. I'll speak my mind."

"Are you done?" Alex asked. "I have to give Luke more information."

"Probably not, but go ahead."

"Luke, you've gotta go to court later today," Alex stated, his voice suddenly sounding formal. "I'll call you and let you know the time, but we also have to deal with your escape. By the way, how did you pull that off?"

"Sorry, I can't tell you."

"Well, anyway, what happens about that will be up to the prosecutor and the judge, and I don't know if that's gonna be dealt with today or later, but the sheriff wanted me to assure you, he'll make damn sure you won't be doin' any more time."

"Damn sure," Jeb added fervently.

"He'd better," Tess barked, "or I'll hire a lawyer myself and sue his sorry butt, and the whole damn, incompetent department."

"Tess, I'm sure that won't be necessary," Alex said, his voice remaining calm, then turning back to Luke, he added, "There's just one thing I've gotta ask. On that first day, did you jump off the train goin' to Longville before it left the station and take off into the woods?" "Yep."

"I knew it!"

"I saw you," Luke said with a grin. "You got real close to me at one point."

"To be honest, I'm glad I didn't find you. We might not be sittin' here if I had."

"No, you wouldn't." Tess declared, "and that horrible woman would still be running around pulling her shit."

"Tess," Jeb said gravely, "you'd better watch your step. We just found a wanted man here at your house."

"Well, my goodness," she said dramatically, throwing up her arms and rolling her eyes. "I'm sure his presence in my living room is doing great injury to the community!"

"You've gotta stop bein' a brat," Jeb retorted. "It's not helpin' you any." "Didn't you just tell me anyone who helped him is off the hook?"

"We still need to know the extent of your involvement," Alex said solemnly. "Just tell us what happened."

"Fine! Luke knocked on my door late last night. It was pouring with rain and I let him in, period. That's it. End of story."

As Jeb and Alex stared at her, Dwayne, who had been sitting on the floor with Rex during the entire exchange, dropped his eyes back to his dog.

"Do you have any evidence to the contrary?" she demanded. "No, I didn't think so, because there isn't any!"

"Besides the diaries, did you find anything else at Patty's cabin?" Luke asked hastily, wanting to change the subject and break the tense moment.

"Yep. She kept a trophy box, and it's sizable," Alex replied. "Several watches are in there. I've no doubt Daniel will identify some them as belongin' to his brother. Are you missin' anything?"

"Yeah. My mom gave me a horse shoe bolo. It's rolled black leather, and the horse shoe is silver. I couldn't for the life of me figure out where I lost it."

"You didn't. When I saw it, I thought it might be yours."

"Damn...I'm kinda speechless," Luke mumbled.

"That's it," Jeb declared, rising to his feet. "Luke, where will you be if I need to reach you?"

"If it's okay with Tess," Luke said with a smile, "I'll be here."

"Sure, Luke, you can say as long as you want," she said sweetly. "The guest room is all yours."

"Tess," Alex said softly, "we're lawmen. We have to follow where the evidence leads us, and we're only human. We all make mistakes."

She paused, then fixing him with a steady gaze, she tilted her head to the side.

"In future, when you're following that evidence, consider the man—or woman—you've got in your crosshairs. If you'd taken the time to learn about Luke, you would've realized he's not capable of attacking an old man. You have to start paying attention and actually listening to people and looking into their hearts. You have to start behaving like people, not robots. You have to start doing what's right!"

A heavy silence descended.

It was Dwayne who was the first to speak.

"Thanks for takin' care of Rex last night," he said, rising to his feet and walking up to her.

"Believe me, it was my pleasure. I love your dog." "I guess I'll be seein' you later today," Luke said, stepping forward and offering his hand.

"Again," Jeb said soberly, shaking it firmly, "we're sorry."

"Real sorry," Alex added, clasping Luke's fingers. "I don't know how we'll make this up to you, but we'll find a way."

Luke walked them to the door and closed it behind them, but Tess remained where she was. She'd said what she'd wanted to, and she had nothing to add.

"That was quite a speech," Luke said softly, ambling over to her and wrapping her up in his arms. "I said it before, and I'll say it again. You really are something special."

"I hate them," she muttered angrily. "I'll never forgive them for what they did."

"Sure you will, and I will too, but it's not gonna happen overnight. In the meantime, we'll take a shower, have some breakfast, and then darlin'..."

CHAPTER TWENTY-FOUR

TESS SAT NERVOUSLY at the kitchen table. Luke had been uncharacteristically quiet over the breakfast. The dishes had been cleaned up and put away, but he remained reserved as he drank the last of his coffee.

"I wish you'd say something," she said softly. "Should I leave?"

"Nope, my thinkin's done, now it's time for you to listen, and I'm gonna warn you right now. Don't interrupt me or give me any of your backtalk. Got it?"

"Yes, definitely," she said earnestly. "I promise I won't say a word."

"Tess," he began solemnly "I love your spirit. The way you spoke to Jeb and Alex took my breath away. They deserved to hear everything you said, and I admire your courage. Damn, Tess, you're fearless, but your willful foolishness, that's just not gonna fly," he said, shaking his head. "You seem to think it's okay to do whatever you want, even when you know better. I gave you a real good spankin' to make it clear you weren't to spend any time with that crazy woman, and what did you do?"

Dropping her eyes, she stared at the table, a hot flush crossing her cheeks.

"Answer the question."

"When she called and asked if we could meet at the cafe for dinner, I agreed."

"What do you think I should do about that? A spankin' didn't stop you, so I guess a spankin' to punish you isn't gonna do much good either."

"I'm sorry, Luke," she whispered. "Whatever you think is best."

"At least that's one lesson you've learned. First, I'm gonna give you two licks with my belt to get your brain focused, then you're gonna kneel in a corner for a while."

The threat sent a flood of wet heat through her sex, but it also made her shudder.

"I want you naked and waitin' for me bent over the bed," he ordered. "I'll be along in a minute."

"Okay."

"Nope, try that again."

"Oh, sorry," she quickly apologized. "Yes, Sir."

Nervously rising from the table, she hurried to her bedroom and anxiously removed her clothes. She was leaning over the side of the bed just as he walked in. Her eyes caught sight of his black leather belt doubled over and hanging from his hand.

"Just two, just like I said," he reminded her, seeing her worried gaze, "but, Tess, only if you ask."

"Ask?" she stammered, staring up at him.

"Yep."

"Uh, please will you, uh, spank me with your belt?" she managed, her stomach churning.

"Are you sure? Don't say yes just cos you think that's what I wanna hear."

Tess closed her eyes.

She was poised to accept the discipline.

She wanted it.

She actually—really—wanted it.

"Yes, Sir, I do," she quivered. "I know what I did was totally wrong, and it caused so much trouble."

"That's good, Tess," he murmured, stepping up and standing at her side.

As he rested the leather across the center of her bottom, she squeezed her eyes shut and took a breath.

She felt it lift, then it suddenly landed with a white hot, stinging heat. Letting out a loud yelp and throwing back her head, she'd barely caught her breath when it struck again.

"Shit, shit, shit," she shouted, stamping her feet. "That really hurts."

Throwing the belt on the bed, he took her by the elbow and led her to the corner of the room.

"Kneel down, close your eyes, put your hands behind your head, and keep 'em there," he directed firmly. "Think real hard about what you did, and why. When I come back, you're gonna tell me everything that went through that willful head of yours. Are we clear?"

"Yes, Sir."

"If you hear a knock at the front door, that's just Robbie droppin' something by for me. You keep your mind focused."

"Yes, Sir."

Letting out a heavy breath as she heard him leave, she closed her eyes and bit her bottom lip. She longed to rub her scalded skin, but she didn't dare. Luke had taken her in hand in no uncertain terms, and in spite of her sorry state, it made her love him even more.

TESS WAS SASSY AS ANY female he'd ever met, and he adored her, but while her unpredictability and courage were part of her charm, they caused her to make reckless decisions and march head first into trouble.

He was on his way to the kitchen for a second cup of coffee when he heard a knock, but he knew Robbie would still be at least ten minutes away. Striding to the door and opening it, he found an attractive young man.

"Hello. You must be Luke Larson. Jeb said I'd find you here. I'm Daniel Griswald. Sorry to arrive unannounced like this. I tried calling earlier but there was no answer."

"Daniel!" Luke exclaimed, shaking his hand. "Unfortunately I only have a minute, but I'm really pleased to meet you. Come in."

"I only have a minute myself," Daniel replied. "I'm heading home to get my brother out of prison, but I couldn't leave without stopping by to thank you. If you hadn't been brave enough to come back to clear your name, I'd still be grasping at straws."

"Hey, Daniel, it goes both ways. It was you who gave Alex what he needed to start diggin'. I am curious though. If he hadn't, how were you plannin' to nail Patty's ass?"

"I wasn't sure, but when I met her she started flirting with me, so I played along. When I was finally at her cabin she made it clear she was into kink. I thought I'd tie her up and blindfold her, then search her house, but I got this weird feelin' and decided to wait until she wasn't around."

"Just as well," Luke remarked. "I'm sure you've heard about her twisted booby traps."

"Are you kidding? Alex and I were almost swallowed up by a fisherman's net wrapped with barbed wire," Daniel replied. "Anyway, thanks, Luke," he continued, pulling out his wallet and withdrawing a card. "If you ever need anything, anything at all, please call me."

"Back at ya, but I don't have a card. I'm listed though."

"Give my love to Tess. She's a remarkable woman."

"Yeah, she is," Luke replied, picturing her on her knees in the bedroom.

"I have to come back, and when I do I'll definitely stop by the cafe."

"I'll let her know, and, uh, tell your brother I know how he's been feelin'," Luke said with a frown, recalling his dark days behind bars. "I'd like to meet him one day. Maybe share a drink and compare notes."

"I think he'd find some comfort in that. Now I really must go. Bye, Luke, and thanks again."

"Bye, Daniel. Safe travels."

Walking him out, and watching him climb into the waiting cab, Luke was about to close the door when Robbie rolled to a stop at the curb and stepped from his truck.

"Here you go," he declared, jogging up the path and handing Luke a brown leather bag.

"Thanks, Robbie. I'll be home tomorrow, and this time I won't be leavin'."

"No shit! That's for certain?"

"That's for certain," Luke said, breaking into a wide smile. "It's over. Well, almost. I've gotta stop by the courthouse later today."

"I'm kinda speechless."

"Yeah, I know the feelin'. Thanks for everything, Robbie. It wouldn't have happened without you."

"I'd do it all again."

"I wouldn't," Luke said with a chuckle. "I'll see you in the mornin'."

"I'll be waitin', and so will Ghost!" Robbie exclaimed, then spontaneously and awkwardly hugging him, he strode away.

Closing the door and still grinning, Luke walked into the living room and settled on the couch. Spinning the dial on the heavy-duty, combination padlock, he opened the bag and stared at his array of wicked toys. Finding the three implements he wanted, he headed back to see Tess.

"Lower your hands," he ordered, entering the bedroom.

Placing two of the items on the nightstand, he carried the third with him. It was a blindfold, and as he placed it over her eyes, he heard her gasp.

"What have you got to say for yourself?" he asked, securing it at the back of her head.

"I'm sorry I didn't listen to you," she replied earnestly. "I broke a promise, several promises, because I thought I knew better. I wanted to help, but I went about it the wrong way and it won't happen again, Sir."

"I'm glad to hear all that, but I have to make sure you've learned your lesson."

Taking her by the elbow and helping her up, he led her to the bed and sat down, but kept her standing.

"You need a serious dose of humility," he declared. "I know you can't see, but you can feel the edge of my legs. Lean forward and lay over my lap."

As she tilted tentatively forward, he guided her over his thighs, then stared down at the two red stripes gracing her ass. She deserved them both, maybe more, but he knew the short, strict discipline had made the desired impact.

"Reach back and give me your hand."

As she moved her arm behind her, he took her wrist and placed her palm on her cheek.

"You say you've learned your lesson. Let's see how obedient you can be. Pull yourself apart and show yourself to me."

"Oooh, Sir."

"Do you wanna say no?"

"I—uh—"

"Your choice. I'll count to three, then pick up my lucky hat and leave. One...two..."

"Wait, stop! I understand why you're doing this," she bleated, and taking a deep breath, she followed his instruction.

"Good girl," he said softly. "Keep it there."

Lifting the small bottle of lube and the dildo from the nightstand, he squeezed a dollop of the slick substance on the tip, then placed it against her forbidden entrance.

"I'm about to insert this, and, Tess, you'll cooperate. I'm countin' to three. One...two...three."

As he pushed it forward, she winced, then sighed deeply, and to his delight she surrendered, allowing the plug to slip into place.

"Humiliating isn't it?"

"Yes, Sir, very."

"Just what a disobedient, willful girl needs. Next time you go ignore my wishes because you think you know better, this is where you'll end up. Are we clear?"

"Ooh, yes, Sir."

"But you'll get four stripes from the belt, spend more time in the corner, and this," he declared, tapping the flange, "will be bigger. You might want to bear that in mind. Now release your cheek and kneel in front of me."

As she dropped her hand away, he helped her off his lap and guided her into position.

"You said you wanted to make things up to me. How do you think you can do that?"

"Uh, pleasure your cock with my mouth, Sir?"

"That's a privilege."

"Of course, sorry, Sir," she said quickly. "If it would please you, I could pleasure your cock with my mouth. Please may I have the honor, Sir?"

"Much better."

Sanding up, he quickly peeled off his jeans, then sat back down and presented his swollen member to her lips.

THOUGH IT WAS UNCOMFORTABLE, Tess couldn't deny the butt plug was having a profound effect. A deep sense of submission flowed through her being. When he gripped her hair to direct her rhythm, she felt herself sink even more deeply into the sublime state.

"Very nice, Tess. This is how a good girl behaves," he murmured. "I'm gonna spank you every Sunday night, and finish it off with that plug. Let's see if that keeps your willful brat under control."

The news sent an erotic fire through her belly, and as he pushed her into a faster pace, she lustily obliged, licking and sucking with unbridled energy.

Drops of pre-come fell on her tongue.

She sensed he was near his climax.

His fingers tightened around her hair, and he slowly withdrew.

"Stroke me with your hand."

Taking hold of his cock, she vigorously moved her grip up and down his shaft. Only moments passed before he groaned deeply and exploded his essence across her fingers.

"That was real good, Tess," he said breathlessly as he removed her blindfold. "Go clean up and bring me back a damp cloth."

"I pleased you?" she asked softly, gazing up at him.

"Yeah, darlin', you sure did."

Moving into the bathroom and washing her hands, she dampened a face cloth and returned to the bedroom, finding him stretched out on his back. Gently wiping him clean, she placed the cloth on the nightstand and laid down beside him.

"Luke, how long do I have to wear this thing?"

"Until I decide to take it out, but it probably won't be long. That phone's gonna ring soon, and I'll have to leave for the court house."

"What a great thing. I need to be there. Please will you let me come?"

"I need you with me too, darlin'," he murmured, sliding his fingers into her pussy and rubbing her clit, "and yeah, you're gonna come, you're gonna come real hard," he growled, kissing his way down her neck to her chest.

"Ooh, thank you…"

"Good girls get rewarded," he muttered, raising his head, "and now you know what happens to bad girls. I won't hesitate to whip your ass if you need it."

His warning sent fresh butterflies fluttering in her stomach, and as he dropped his mouth to her nipples and hungrily drew them in, she could feel her orgasm looming.

"Damn, you're wet," he grunted, pausing to glance up at her, "so fuckin' wet."

Suddenly thrusting two fingers into her drenched channel, he urgently moved them in and out.

The orgasm rose up inside her.

She held her breath.

Her back arched.

The dam broke.

Letting out a wild cry, she was swept away by the spasms shuddering through her body. Wave after wave of tingling sensations fired through her limbs, until finally waning, they left her limp in his arms. Floating in the post-orgasmic bliss, she was barely aware of him removing the unwanted intruder.

SILENT MINUTES TICKED by. When Tess finally stirred, Luke hugged her tightly, then propped himself up on an elbow.

"Hey, darlin'. How are you feelin'?"

"Relieved—happy—and sore of course. What about you?"

"Just relieved and happy," he replied with a grin. "Hey, Tess, I've been thinkin'. When I was arrested we were just gettin' off the ground, but we both knew it was special."

"I sure did, but I let people—"

"Shush," he said softly, placing his finger on her lips. "The night I walked into the cafe, I was bettin' on what you knew in your heart, but I had no inklin' you and I would become so close so quick."

"It has been kind of a whirlwind, but I'm not complaining, not for a second."

"'Neither am I, and considerin' how we just spent the last hour, and you've got a weekly spankin' comin', what I'm gonna say next might sound a bit strange, but Tess, I wanna go back to courtin' you like I was before all the trouble."

"Luke, that sounds so romantic. I would love it, though I'm not sure we'll be able to settle for a goodnight kiss at the door."

"You might be right about that," he said with a chuckle, "and maybe we won't, but I'll be livin' at the ranch, and you'll be here. I wanna take you out, and spend dinners learnin' all about you. Let's do this thing right."

"That sounds perfect."

Lowering his head, he lovingly lingered his mouth on hers, then slowly pulled back.

"There, sealed with a kiss," he said softly. "After we leave the courtroom, we'll go to that Italian place just outta town and celebrate, then come back here and I'll stay the night, but I'll head back to the ranch in the mornin'. Then, darlin'," he said, pausing dramatically, "you'll have to wait for your phone to ring."

"Uh-huh," she murmured with a sassy grin, "and you'll have to hope I'll answer!"

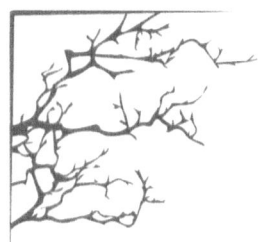

EPILOGUE

NOT ONLY WAS LUKE EXONERATED, those in the small town who had condemned him went out of their way to apologize. When they learned that he had been largely responsible for exposing a dangerous woman living in their midst, he was labeled a hero.

The Mayor gave him the key to the city, Tess's father welcomed him into his home, and the Anderson's offered him the use of the Lodge whenever he wanted to use it. The black wool jacket Tess had borrowed from the lodge turned out to be Tyler's. He jokingly declared it should remain at the luxury cabin in case it was ever needed for such an occasion again, then insisted she keep it.

Daniel's powerful father made sure the news of his son's innocence hit the headlines. The story quickly spread and became national news. In just a few days Jeb and Alex were fielding calls from detectives and defense attorneys with questions about the woman named Patty Jamison, aka Jamie Patterson. It was soon discovered she was wanted in several states, and more incarcerated victims of her evil cunning were uncovered. To everyone's surprise, several rewards posted in various states for her arrest and conviction.

Though Daniel was invited to take an equal share of the unexpected windfall along with Luke, Tess and Robbie, he already had a generous trust fund, and insisted it be split between the three of them. Luke paid off his mortgage, Robbie, took care of the loan against his truck and put the balance into a savings account, and Tess was thrilled at the prospect of remodeling her cafe. Throwing herself into the job with a vengeance, she demolished the storage room and built a patio for outdoor dining. The freezer took center stage as a large flower bed, with an ornate brass plaque dedicating it to Luke Larson.

But when all facts came out, and the extent of Dwayne's involvement were exposed, the Sheriff had to ask for his resignation.

"I have no choice, boy," he'd declared. "I can't have it known that my nephew was aiding and abetting a wanted felon, even if the criminal in question turned out not to be a criminal after all."

Standing in his uncle's office, Dwayne pretended to be disappointed, but he was overjoyed. The very next day he was hired by the local animal shelter, and quickly nicknamed, Dwayne Doolittle.

LUKE KEPT HIS PROMISE.

Tess received flowers and cards, he whisked her away to romantic retreats, and even after the thirty-days had passed, he continued to spank her every Sunday night, with a follow-up visit from the dreaded butt plug.

Late one night when they were snuggling in bed, she asked him how he'd managed to escape from the penitentiary.

"It's how I got this scar," he said gravely, touching his right eyebrow. "There was a fight in the canteen. One of the nastiest men in there smashed a bottle and was goin' for a guard who had his back turned. I jumped in and stopped him just as he was about to cut the guy's throat."

"Oh, my gosh! Luke! You could've been killed! What were you thinking?"

"I wasn't. I just reacted. Anyway, long story short, the guard and I became friends. When I told him why I was in there, he decided he was gonna help me get out so I could make things right—especially with you."

"You're such an amazing man," she murmured, wrapping her arms around him and hugging him tightly. "I love you to pieces."

The weeks became months, spring was upon them, and he made arrangements to spend the weekend at the Anderson's Lodge. When she arrived at his ranch, she found Dusty tacked up and waiting for the picturesque trek.

"I'm so happy we're going back there," she said gratefully, pecking him on the cheek.

"The weather's gonna be perfect, and I'll take you on that picnic I promised."

"That sounds wonderful. I can't wait."

"And I have a few other surprises," he said with a wink.

"I'll just bet you do, and maybe I have something planned as well," she said with a giggle, thinking about the puppy she and Dwayne had picked out, "but my surprise will be waiting for you when we get back." "Why didn't you just bring it with you?"

"You'll find out," she replied with a sassy grin. "Tell me more about this picnic. Where will we go?"

"The meadow above the lake. We'll drink wine, eat chocolates, watch the sunset, and then..."

"And then what?"

"And then we'll have to see," he said softly, and dropping his hand in his pocket, he nervously wrapped his fingers around the small, black, velvet box.

Dear Reader:
Thank you for buying this book. If you have a moment I would greatly appreciate
your review. I constantly strive to bring you interesting and enjoyable content and your
feedback is valued. Feel free to contact me at any time. I love to hear from readers. My
email is: MagCarpenter@yahoo.com, and here are my social media links should you care
to check them out.

My very best wishes,

Maggie

http://www.MaggieCarpenter.com
https://www.facebook.com/MaggieCarpenterWriter
https://twitter.com/magcarpenter2

BOOKS BY MAGGIE CARPENTER

WESTERN ROMANCE
ROUGH COWBOY
HUNKS and HORSES
A Four Book Series Each HEA and Standalone
TO KISS A COWBOY
TO CATCH A COWBOY
TO CON A COWBOY
TO TRUST A COWBOY
(and more...)
SEXY SCIFI - PARANORMAL
ROUGH ALPHA
TRAINED BY THE ALIEN
WARLOCK
THE ALIEN'S RULES
(and more...)
BDSM CONTEMPORARY ROMANCE
THE STRICT BRITISH BARRISTER
SINS BEHIND THE SCENES:
I AM A DOMINANT:
DESIRE UNLEASHED - Sexsomnia.
TIMELESS OBSESSION
(and more...)
For a full list of her novels visit her author page.
https://www.amazon.com/author/maggiecarpenter[1]

---

1. https://www.amazon.com/authormaggiecarpenter